Annie Thomas

Utterly mistaken

Vol. II

Annie Thomas

Utterly mistaken
Vol. II

ISBN/EAN: 9783337054571

Printed in Europe, USA, Canada, Australia, Japan

Cover: Foto ©Andreas Hilbeck / pixelio.de

More available books at **www.hansebooks.com**

UTTERLY MISTAKEN.

A Novel.

BY

ANNIE THOMAS

(Mrs. Pender Cudlip),

AUTHOR OF

"DENIS DONNE," "THE HONBLE. JANE,"

Etc, Etc.

IN THREE VOLUMES.

VOL. II.

LONDON:

F. V. WHITE & CO.,

31, SOUTHAMPTON STREET, STRAND, W.C.

1893.

PRINTED BY
KELLY AND CO. LIMITED, GATE STREET, LINCOLN'S INN FIELDS
AND KINGSTON-ON-THAMES.

CONTENTS.

UTTERLY MISTAKEN.

UTTERLY MISTAKEN.

CHAPTER I.

BOUND FOR TRELYN.

THE time of roses was long past. A glorious autumn had followed a lovely summer, and winter was behaving itself properly with regard to snow, sharp frosts, and excellent skating. Young men of light and leading were driving tandem over the Serpentine, and an ox had been roasted whole on the Thames. Christmas was upon us— Christmas with all its holy, pure associations created by God, and also with many that are neither pure nor holy created by man. But still in spite of this latter fact a time for the renewal of many a broken tie, and of a general gathering together of families and friends.

To begin with the least important of the players who are strutting on the little stage before us.

Mrs. Robert Davis and her children had found an asylum in a pretty old thatched house belonging to Sir Walter St. Austle, and standing midway between Trelyn Towers and a little country town. Here they lived on a small income, the children in blissful ignorance of their sadly pauperised and worse than fatherless condition, the wife in a perfectly unauthorised state of equally blissful certainty of "hearing from poor Robert very soon, and of being able to hold up her head with the highest again."

Meantime "poor Robert" was still leading the life of a well-stalled and fed ox in the sequestered nook in Norwood which he had chosen as his hiding-place. And having the satisfaction the while of seeing that he was being much sought for in America, Australia, Monte Carlo, various parts of India, and even in "far Japan."

Sir Walter and Lady St. Austle had settled down at Trelyn Towers immediately after their marriage, and Laura had borne the blow of finding that she did not bring a penny to her husband, but, on the other hand, owed a considerable amount of money which he had to pay, with exquisite equanimity. On the other hand, it must be conceded that she bore with equal equanimity the sad story of his losses on the turf and in his training stables.

18*

The pain of living on a small income in a large place never seemed to affect Laura at all, while to her husband it was gall and bitterness. She was very happy in her beautiful home, and never felt a pang at not being able to fill it with guests. She was always well served and waited upon, therefore the cutting down of the establishment which Sir Walter found necessary did not affect her. Both her health and her temper were perfect in fact, and the only trouble she had in life was the thought that sometimes crossed her mind that "poor Robert, who had always been so good to her," might be wanting something. When this thought arose she would cry for a few minutes, and then go and give some presents to his children, or ask his wife to stay for a day or two at Trelyn, during which time she would heap every kindness and attention she could upon that forlorn and faithful woman, and perhaps feel a little hurt at Anna's so palpably taking for granted all that was done for her, and obviously expecting more.

But these were the only crumples in Laura's rose-leaf, and in the midst of many a monetary trouble that beset him about this period Sir Walter found her so soothing that he would have done the deed of "marrying her again, even had he known her to be penniless when he did so."

Can the magnificent generosity of man go beyond such a declaration as this? especially when he is hard up himself.

Mrs. Poynter and Ella were still "so near" in their pretty house in Kensington, and still as far as the poles asunder in affec-

tion and sympathy, as at the time of Laura
Davis's marriage.   Guy St. Austle had gone
out to Australia with his new play, which
had been so judiciously boomed that he was
expected home shortly with his pockets full
of money.   And when he came Mrs.
Poynter knew that she would have to
decide at once and for ever as to his future
and her own.

The loss of him during all these months,
after having been so closely and sweetly
intimate with him for so many weeks, had
taught her a truth.   He was so much to
her, her longing for him, for his companion-
ship, for his advice, for his opinions, for his
sympathy, for *himself*, was so intense that
she knew she could never live the best
that was in life without him.

"If Ella would only marry and relieve me

of the responsibility I feel about her, I would lay aside all my morbid fears and make Guy and myself happy," she often thought. But then a shadow thrown by the mere thought of Ella would darken her mind and judgment, and she would turn aside from the contemplation of her own possible happiness, and wistfully consider how best she could fulfil her responsibilities towards the girl who had neither father nor mother to turn to, and who was always ready to develop wasp-like qualities towards the one to whose charge she had been consigned, and on whom she was utterly dependent.

It was not a case of " no one coming to marry, no one coming to woo " that left Ella in maiden meditation still. An excellent opportunity of settling herself in com-

fort down as the wife of a rising young
Kensington doctor was open to her. But
the girl was not fancy free. Her fancy
had been caught by Guy St. Austle. Her
heart had followed her fancy, as does
sometimes happen even with the most
frivolous of her sex. And now it had
come to this, that she would stop at
nothing short of a crime to detach him
from her step-mother and win him to herself. Accordingly it may easily be con-
ceived that she was looking forward to his
return with quite as much impatient
anxiety as Mabel Poynter herself was ex-
periencing. This impatient anxiety the
girl had to conceal, as she lived in dread of
Mrs. Poynter's discovering and thwarting
it. Ella no longer proclaimed the admiration she felt for Guy St. Austle by planting

miniatures of him painted by herself about the house in every direction. But her step-mother had a shrewd suspicion that one lurked in Ella's pocket, while another kept guard over her girlish slumbers every night.

That these two women were desperately jealous of one another about Mr. St. Austle was an indisputable fact, and though one had a right to feel the humiliating passion on his account, while the other had not the faintest shadow of one to plead in justification of her folly, they suffered from it to the same extent.

Mrs. Poynter had the right, for Guy had told her how well he loved her a hundred times, and a hundred times had pleaded for her love in return. Whereas to Ella he had never shown any feeling stronger than that demanded by courtesy towards the most casual acquaintance. But the girl had taken an interest in him just out of revengeful, suspicious hatred. This had turned to hungry, jealous love, when she had discovered that her suspicions and her revenge were alike uncalled for. It stung her to distraction when she recalled looks which she had seen him give, and words which she had heard him speak to her step-mother! "Would she (Ella) ever win similar ones from him?" she asked herself restlessly a thousand times in the course of the week that was to bring him back to England. That she would have a chance of testing her powers in his direction soon she knew. For Mrs. Poynter and herself were invited down to spend a fortnight at Trelyn in January, and Guy "would be

there," Lady St. Austle had said in her
letter. In the freedom of country-house
life she would have opportunities of being
with him that would be denied to her older
step-mother. Ella gloated over those years
which Mrs. Poynter possessed in addition to
those owned by Ella herself. It galled her
horribly to have to admit to herself that her
step-mother's figure and points compared
favourably with her own. It annoyed
the girl greatly to see that the simplest style
of dress looked no more incongruously
youthful on Mrs. Poynter's graceful form
than if she had been eighteen.

"But she must go to pieces soon," Miss
Poynter tried to console herself by thinking;
"in two or three years she'll have to say
good-bye to the thirties, and then she'll
stoop or get broad and look quite matronly

and uninteresting, while he will look young
and handsome as ever. Besides, it's *awful*
that he should be tricked into taking
another man's leavings. Oh, how *could*
poor dear Papa forgive the creature and
leave his money to her, after once having
found her out?"

So the apparently guileless young girl
plotted and planned the downfall and disgrace of a woman who had never been
anything but kind to her. And with that
criminating letter which she had found
among her father's private papers safely
locked up in her dressing-case, Miss Poynter
went down with the unsuspecting Mabel to
stay at Trelyn Towers and meet Guy St.
Austle.

*   *   *   *   *

Preparations for paying a visit to the

same place at the same time were simultaneously being made in the pretty little Norwood cottage in which Robert Davis, under the name of Denham, had taken sanctuary.

"I've met an old chum, a fellow I knew at Harrow, St. Austle, a Cornish baronet, with a lot of dollars," Ted Greg told his wife excitedly one day, coming into the still, subdued life of the little cottage like a strong northerly wind sweeping all before it.

He had been away from home about a fortnight, staying with some relations in the North—relations who were glad to have him in the hunting season because he was a first-rate man after the hounds, and showed off their hunters (at two hundred guineas a-piece) in a way they were unequal to themselves. They found he organised their big shoots admirably also, for he was as good with a gun as with a horse. And as he had pulled the biggest salmon out of the river that ran through their grounds which had ever been landed in the district, he and his rod were always welcome during the open season. But his wife had never been asked to accompany him!

It was the old, old story. She had loved him not wisely but too well, and when she had lost her husband, home, position, honour, means of subsistence, and reputation for his sake, he had acted "honourably," all his friends said, in marrying her. The truth being that he performed this honourable act because he had got into the habit of being adored by her, and knew that no other woman would wait upon him so untiringly, unselfishly, and well.

From the very first he had never permitted the marriage tie to weigh heavily
upon him. Fashionáble people, his own
relations, even people who were intensely
moral to all outward appearances, forgave
handsome, swaggering Ted Greg his share
in the found-out sin very quickly, but they
did not extend their leniency to his wife.
They ignored her as something quite outside their virtuous ken, and fell into the
way of speaking of "poor Ted" as if she
were the only offender in the case.

She accepted her position as a proud
woman, who had been pure as an angel
until her overwhelming love for this one
man caused her to trip, is sure to accept it.
That is to say, she bore every slight un-
flinchingly, never showing the pain she felt,
never reproaching him, but just patiently

sinking into obscurity, and devoting all her energies to serving him.

It never occurred to him to think that she had made a huge sacrifice for him. He thought lightly of women ; his previous experiences had been among the loosest of their sex, and when poor Marian Poynter bowed her pride and perilled her soul for his sake, he took it quite in the order of things and never suspected that she suffered martyrdom for her frailty.

"St. Austle has asked me to go down to his place in Cornwall for a fortnight, he can give me very good snipe - shooting and mount me if the frost doesn't stop the hunting," Mr. Greg went on cheerfully.

" Dear Ted, I must—" she hesitated and then finished her sentence in a way she had not intended doing when she began it :

"What day do you go?"

"On the tenth; by-the-way, you must get me some new stockings, I'm tired of the black and grey. Get them fawn-coloured ground with darker brown diamonds on them. I ought to have some new white shirts. Those infernal laundresses at Laxby jagged the cuffs and fronts frightfully."

"Can you give me any money, Ted?"

"What a woman you are! Why didn't you ask me for it before? I'm cleared out, at least I must keep enough to take me down to Trelyn and tip the gamekeepers and grooms. What do you do with the money that old fossil pays you for the rooms?"

"Pay the rent and live on it," she said quietly.

He knitted his brows thoughtfully for a

few moments, then his countenance cleared up wonderfully as he suggested :

" Why not let another bed and sitting-room at two guineas a week ? you'd be in clover then ? "

" This is the only other sitting-room."

" Well, I'm rarely at home, and you don't use it much, I suppose ; you seem to me to spend most of your time doing the slavey's work in the kitchen."

" I only do that when you are at home, because you won't eat what she cooks," she said, gently, whereupon he got angry and said she " was always trying to make him out to be a selfish and unreasonable brute."

" Ted, dear Ted, don't say that," she gasped, going over and bending down to kiss the handsome face, which still had the power to make her thrill through every fibre of her being when it beamed affectionately upon her. She had been his wife for fifteen years and still he was her hero! No other man had ever stirred the pulses or touched the warm heart of Marian Greg but this careless, debonair, selfish, attractive, unworthy husband of hers.

He permitted her to caress him, and even took the trouble to put his arm round her waist and draw her down to his knee. But he was not thinking of her even while he did these things, she felt sure of that. His mind had reverted to the visit he was going to pay to his old friend, Sir Walter St. Austle, and to a casual consideration of the means of getting the things it would be needful for him to take with him. He always dressed well, and was fastidious about the look of his luggage, travelling rugs, and toilet appointments. Not in a fussy, feminine way, but in a broad, masculine manner that proclaimed expense was no object.

In various ways Mr. Greg made a lot of money, but he always spent a little more than he made. The false step he had taken in his youth of not only coveting, but taking away his neighbour's wife, was an irretrievable one and had spoilt his career to a great extent. Still he always managed to keep his head above water and to make a fair appearance, and none of his fine friends had an idea that his wife led a joyless, colourless, hard-working life at home. Even had they suspected this truth the majority of them would have said, "Oh, well, what can a woman expect who marries such a devil-may-care chap as Ted Greg? No woman with a grain of sense could ever have expected him to settle down to domestic felicity in a quiet way."

It may be told here that his wife had long ceased to entertain any such unreasonable expectation. But she loved him just as blindly, passionately and pardoningly as she had done when she gave up the world for love

CHAPTER II.

THE play which Guy St. Austle had produced first in Australia achieved such a distinguished success, made in the slang of the day " such a big boom," that he had no difficulty in getting the manager of " The Comet" to accept and promise to produce it without delay as soon as he returned to England. It was put into rehearsal even before he went down to Trelyn. If it had not been for the joyful certainty he had that Mabel Poynter would be a fellow-guest with him at his brother's place, he would have found it impossible to tear himself away from the fascination of daily witnessing the efforts of an intelligent company to get inside his characters. As it was he felt he might with safety leave them to the direction of the stage manager for a fortnight, while he tackled the far more difficult task of getting inside Mrs. Poynter's character and discovering what was her real motive for holding him at arms' length.

He never doubted or distrusted her love for him. A man never does when a woman has once shown that he, and he only, has stirred her heart to its depths. But he did distrust her judgment about him. He thought that she had taken alarm at the wild, very much variegated life he had been compelled by circumstances to lead. He knew that women very often do entertain the notion, that unless a man is

married he must of necessity get into a
love-scrape in every outlandish corner of
the world in which he may be thrust by
Fate.   Without being what men term a
saint, Guy St. Austle was a remarkably
clean-handed man, and it hurt him to think
that Mrs. Poynter might be suspicious of
him.   In thinking that she was this, he
himself was guilty of injustice, for Mrs.
Poynter believed too firmly in the power of
her own ascendancy over him to imagine
for a moment that he had ever been tricked
into error by love for any other woman.

Mrs. Poynter and her step-daughter went
down to Trelyn on the same day, but not
by the same train as Guy. She and Ella
started at nine o'clock from Paddington,
whereas he waited to see a rehearsal at two
o'clock of his play, and travelled by the

night train. If she had been alone the rehearsal would not have been benefited by his presence and instructions. But the fact of Ella being with her made him resign the privilege of ministering to Mabel's wants on the long, tedious journey.

Once or twice during his absence in Australia he had received gentle reminders of this girl's existence. Once she had sent him, merely with her compliments, several press-cuttings containing notices of his latest novel. At another time she had tried to tickle his vanity by sending him a delicately painted miniature of himself, with the words " painted from memory " written in a scroll formed of forget-me-nots on the back. To these attentions he had responded promptly but not warmly, for he began to fear that he might be subjected to a series of them when he returned to England, and to be continually called upon to recognise them would take up too much time. He tried to keep the idea at bay that Ella was honouring him with a warmer feeling than he desired to win from her. At the same time he remembered that she had become watchful and jealous of Mrs. Poynter before he went to Australia, and the receipt of the press notices and the likeness of himself showed that she had not forgotten him by any means.

Before they had been at Trelyn two days he found himself very much harassed by the continual little onslaughts the girl made upon him. She was perpetually wanting his opinion about a picture or a poem or a new novel, and she would always seek for this opinion when he was alone. The frost continued sternly, there was no hunting, and the whole party spent most of their time on the ice, some skating, and others who were not proficient in that graceful art being pushed about comfortably in chairs. Mrs. Poynter belonged to this latter class, and Guy St. Austle devoted himself to her service, until Ella hinted that he had given her to understand that " he found it a great bore to be kept dancing attendance on people who had no business on the ice unless they could skate and look after themselves."

When she heard that, poor Mabel froze up nearly as hard as the surface of the lake itself, and would have no more of his help, humbly as he proffered it. While Ella, finding the first sowing of malicious seed bore fruit so speedily, threw about a handful or two more broadcast.

"I hope when I'm quite old—as old as Mrs. Poynter—that I shall not be silly and vain and anxious to attract attention," she said one morning when she had followed Guy into the billiard-room and prettily expressed surprise at finding him there.

"What makes you breathe such a worthy but unnecessary aspiration?" he asked.

"Because I can't help seeing that Mrs. Poynter is as eager for the fray as if she had not married and had lovers years ago," Ella replied, lifting her lovely, appealing eyes to his, but speaking with cool hardihood.

"Mrs. Poynter commands attention, she never need be anxious to attract it," he said coldly.

"You admire her so much, do you?" Ella questioned. "Well," she went on spitefully, "I can only tell you that I heard Sir Walter telling her at breakfast this morning before *you* came down, lazy man! that his old chum, "handsome Ted Greg, was coming here to stay," and she coloured up like a girl, and then she asked, "Is he married? is his wife coming with him?" Now how can it possibly concern her whether he's married or not, unless, hearing him called handsome Ted Greg, she wants to get up a flirtation with him?"

Ella brought her argument to a close triumphantly, but Guy looked inexpressibly disgusted.

"Mrs. Poynter is as incapable of 'flirting' as she is of doing anything else vulgar or underhand," he said shortly.

And Ella laughed scornfully as she replied :

"You think so? how I *hate* to see you taken in by her cool, stand-off ways. They're only put on to make you more eager. 'Incapable of flirting or anything else mean or underhand,' is she? Shall I show you a letter that will prove conclusively even to you that she is capable of all the things you mention? Ah! and of worse things too!"

The girl shivered with the force of her own bitter animus. She tried to think that it was loyalty to her dead father which made her pant to unmask the pretender to a seat on Honour's throne, but all the while she knew that she would have let her purpose slip had it not been for the fierce desire that filled her to detach

Guy from Mrs. Poynter and annex him to herself.

"Show me a letter that is not addressed to myself! and that you think would be calculated to lower my esteem for as perfect a woman as the world holds! No, thank you, Miss Poynter."

"Your 'perfect woman' broke my father's heart; if he hadn't been as nearly 'perfect' as a man can be she would have been disgraced. As it was he forgave her and trusted her again, and now she is taking you in. It makes me half mad to see such cunning on one side and such credulity on the other."

The girl spoke with rapidity and concentrated force. Her words cut him like a sharp two-edged sword, but he did not credit them for a moment. Ella's first open attempt to deface the character of the woman he loved was a failure. But Ella had not only passion on her side, she had perseverance and pertinacity also. She had a love as well as a hate to gratify, and for the gratification of one or other of these passions she felt that her strength would be as the strength of ten when obstacles arose in her path.

For the present she was baffled by Guy's composure. All he said when she had finished her tirade was:

"How awfully mistaken you must be! Are you coming down to the lake? I promised to meet Laura and Mrs. Poynter there at twelve."

Ella was clever enough to accept a temporary defeat without making any futile bluster about it. She banished all traces of angry excitement from her face, agreed cheerfully to go down to the lake with him, and after a few minutes' absence reappeared in a short crimson skating dress liberally trimmed with fur, in which she looked like a gorgeous little foreign bird.

She diplomatically avoided making any reference to the subject of their late discussion as they walked briskly down to the lake. But a slight thrill of exultation passed over her as she advanced into the little crowd assembled on the bank with Guy by her side, and Lady St. Austle said laughingly :

"Have you been keeping Guy, or has Guy been keeping you? There have been a thousand enquiries after you both. Walter told me to tell you, Guy, that he relies on you to-day to see that all the

ladders and ropes are in good working
order as he can't be here, and he made me
vow I wouldn't go on unless you could look
after me.   I told him it was rather a
shame to tie you to your sister when there
are so many pretty girls to look after."

Her hand was tucked under Mrs.
Poynter's arm, and Laura felt that arm
twitch as she spoke of the pretty girls.

"The darling!" Lady St. Austle
thought remorsefully, for she was very
loyal to this new friend of hers, Guy's
real love! "She needn't have a pang about
one of the girls, there's not one to whom she
mightn't give points and beat them by her
charm, Walter says. But that step-daughter
knows how to flatter men, and Guy is only
a man."

"Let me run you round on a chair,"

Guy was saying at the same time to Mrs. Poynter.

"No, I mean to be a spectator only to-day. You must look after Lady St. Austle and Ella."

"To-morrow that Admirable Crichton Mr. Greg will be here to divide the labour with you, Guy," Lady St. Austle put in cheerfully. Involuntarily as the name was mentioned, Guy glanced at Mrs. Poynter and saw that her face had grown chalky white. In another moment, becoming conscious that Ella's eyes were fixed upon her as well, she flushed painfully and turned to walk away.

"What on earth could it all mean? Unmistakably Mabel was agitated at the mention of this man Greg's name. Could it be possible that she, proud, pure, perfect

20*

Mabel, could have been indiscreet?" These thoughts would force themselves into Guy's mind, but he dismissed them peremptorily and without trusting himself to meet Ella's eyes, in which he felt tolerably sure an expression of mocking triumph would be lurking, he knelt down to fasten on that young lady's skates.

It has been already said that Mr. St. Austle had no tender feeling whatever for the pretty little girl who was doing her utmost to excite one in him, and artlessly showing her cards the while. But he was not blind to her attractions. Her lustrous eyes, purple lakes of soul-sentiment, intense feeling and slumbering passion, were eyes that not one man in a hundred could look into and remain utterly unmoved. Guy was not the one man in the hundred. Nor was he blind to the beauty of the small slim feet, to which he was affixing the skates.

"They look too slender to support even such a feather weight as you are," he said, when he had finished his task, and Ella looked at them complacently as she replied:

"My feet and hands are an inheritance from my mother, I've been told. She was a great beauty and a finer, taller woman than I am; but my old nurse used to tell me that I had my mother's hands and feet and eyes and hair."

"Have you a likeness of her?" Guy asked. He was involuntarily interested in this unknown woman, of whom her daughter spoke with rapturous fervour, though she could not remember her.

She had got on the ice now and was going round in an intricate figure that displayed her skill and the perfect control she had over her flying feet admirably. As he spoke she checked her graceful progress abruptly and held her hand out to him for support.

"No, I have no portrait of her. I wonder Papa hadn't one taken, for he adored her so. But you see she must have died before he had time to think of everything, for I was only four or five when she 'passed away from us,' as nurse used to call it."

She was in the midst of her explanation, clinging to his hand and looking up into his face with pretty pathetic interest when Mrs. Poynter came up and stood close to them on the bank. She heard Ella's last sentence and knew at once of whom she was speaking.

"Poor girl! may she never know the

truth," Mrs. Poynter thought, pityingly. "Oh, that that man were not coming! A careless word from him may batter down the wall of secrecy that has been so carefully built up round Ella all her life, and reveal a truth that will crush her to the ground. What a goose I am, though, to speak as if it were impossible there should be more than one handsome Ted Greg in the world!"

Mabel looked so mournful as these anxious tender thoughts chased one another through her mind, that Ella said in her heart:

"She is beginning to see that the man she has made so sure of has eyes for other people after all. How I *wish* he would let me show him that letter."

Presently she skimmed away, followed by

a string of the youth of the neighbourhood, for all the families in the region round availed themselves of the frozen lake and of the open house and hospitality which was the order of the day at Trelyn. A number of men came down daily from the Plymouth garrison also, so the gathering was a large and lively one, and the noise they were making drowned the sound of an ominous cracking which only some of those who were standing on the bank heard.

These latter raised an alarm immediately, but Ella did not see clearly the precise direction in which the onlookers were endeavouring to indicate where the danger was. She struck for the bank at the nearest point, but before she reached it the ice cracked, broke asunder, and the girl went down, feet foremost, luckily, into at least twelve feet of water.

Then arose a shout, almost a roar of horror, and fifty voices were raised in giving fifty orders, which no one thought of obeying. In the midst of the turmoil Guy kept his head, and, with the help of another man, ran a ladder from the bank across the chasm to the firm ice beyond. Ella's head appeared simultaneously, and, exhausted as she was, she managed to cling on to the jagged edge of the ice until the ladder was gently shifted to within her reach. By its aid she managed to drag her poor, perishing, fainting, drenched little form to within Guy St. Austle's grasp, and as he clutched her closely to him, she felt that she was having her reward for being half-drowned and nearly frightened to death.

"If you *could* run to the house it would be better for you," he whispered ; but she shook her head, and her pale lips murmured a faint negative to the proposal.

"She can't stand," he explained to the bystanders, "so I must run home with her as fast as I can. One of you fellows rush on and order a hot bath and blankets to be ready when we get there."

Half-a-dozen fellows were off at once in the service of the pretty little icy maiden, beneath whose frozen breast a hot little heart was beating with passionate pleasure at finding Guy's arms clasped so closely round her. His burden was not a heavy one by any means, still, at the pace he was going, it was not expedient for him to waste any of his breath in words. Accordingly, when Ella, with her arms round his neck and her cheek touching his, whispered: "You've saved my life! how I shall always love you for it!" the only reply he made was to incline his head a little nearer to hers and give her a sympathetic hug.

Mrs. Poynter was at the Towers almost as soon as Guy and his charge, and Ella, after being duly parboiled, dosed with hot negus, and laid in a warm bed, speedily recovered her circulation and spirits. The only temporary inconvenience she felt, in fact, was that her step-mother insisted on sitting by her in order to minister to any of her possible wants. This disturbed the easy flow of those lovely memories she was having of that blissful time she had passed in Guy's arms with her cheek resting against his. She had been weak and faint, draggled and weary, her body had been one mass of pains and aches from the cold! but for all that the time had been the most blissful one of her life. She would never forget it. Would he remember it as vividly, she wondered, when next they met?

The following day she heard that Mr. Greg—handsome Ted Greg—had arrived in time to join them at breakfast, "and," Lady St. Austle added, "he was most sincerely cut up when he heard what a narrow escape you've had. He looked absolutely stunned for a moment, didn't he, Mrs. Poynter?"

"I didn't look at him," Mrs. Poynter said coldly—"ungraciously," Ella thought.

CHAPTER III.

HANDSOME Ted Greg very rarely troubled himself about anyone or anything, unless he or his interests were likely to be affected by one or the other. But when he heard that a widowed Mrs. Poynter and her step-daughter Ella were his fellow-guests, and that the girl had narrowly escaped drowning on the previous day, he betrayed a good deal of inexplicable and genuine emotion. Even when he recovered himself, he seemed abstracted and almost gloomy, recalling his attention with an effort and a start when he was addressed, and being apparently in a state of indecision and perplexity.

Guy had seen the first meeting between Mabel Poynter and the new arrival. The lady had bowed very coolly when Mr. Greg had been introduced to her, but had certainly shown no sign of recognition of him, and it was equally evident that the lady was absolutely unknown to the man. Still, her name obviously was known to him, and when he was told of Ella's accident his face grew livid.

In vain Guy conjectured and hunted about for a reason for this consciousness. He could find none, he could think of none; and he shrank from asking Mabel to help him to unravel the mystery. After all, it was no business of his; Mabel was the only person with whom he had to concern himself, and it was clear that, personally, Mr. Greg and Mabel were strangers to each other.

Moodily and meditatively for an hour after breakfast that day Ted Greg sat before the writing-table in his bedroom, a pen in his hand and a cigarette in his mouth, trying to determine whether or not he should write and tell his wife that Mrs. Poynter and her step-child Ella were staying in the same house with him. He very rarely did write to Mrs. Greg when he was away from her, not even when he was staying with people who were well aware of there being a Mrs. Greg at home. This negligence concerning one of the primary duties of an absent spouse arose not from want of love for or indifference about her, but out of a rooted distaste for the art of writing, and an equal distaste to making the Mrs. Greg who had not been invited to accompany

him subject matter for the gossip of
the servants who took the letters to the
post. He did not resent her being
ignored by the old friends and acquaintances who held out the hearty hand of
welcome to him still. But he did shrink
angrily from the idea of her being canvassed
by those whom he was in the habit of
describing colloquially as " their beastly
flunkeys and slaveys."

There had been no necessity for mentioning Marian, or for alluding to the fact
of his being married at all when he had
accidentally met Sir Walter St. Austle, and
been given the invitation to Trelyn Towers.
There would be a certain amount of
awkwardness in bringing this unknown wife
of his upon the *tapis* now. He loved her
dearly when she was near him to be loved.

But when he was away from her he shrank
from doing anything that might cause either
her or himself to be canvassed and conjectured about. So now as the St. Austles
knew nothing whatever about her and did
not suspect the existence of a wife in the
background, he resolved not to write to her
from Trelyn, and just to let matters take
their course with regard to the Poynters.

Whenever he flung aside a half-framed
determination to do anything, and settled to
let things take their course, he relapsed into
his normal state of " sufficient for the day
is the evil thereof," and never troubled himself about any contingency or consequence
that was not immediately under his nose.
Accordingly, now, with the burnt-out end
of his sixth cigarette, he cast aside all care
or consideration for anything outside the

pleasure of the hour.   To the delight of
every light-hearted man and woman the
frost had broken up, and the Scorrier hounds
were to meet on the first open day at
Trelyn.   With such a prospect before him
it was clearly his first duty to get hold of
St. Austle and inspect the stables.

"I hope none of these women hunt?" he
thought, ungallantly but honestly; "unless
they can take care of themselves they're
a cursed nuisance in the field.   Besides, I
hate giving a woman a lead in a strange
country, and one of them's safe to want me
to do it if they're a hunting lot."

He was not misled by his vanity in
saying this.   Handsome, debonair Ted Greg
was as much bothered and beguiled by
women in all directions now as he had
been twenty years ago, when he committed

the fatal folly of his life. Even sensible, prudent women of thirty, and perhaps a few years over, in ignorance of the existence of that handsome, patient, hardworking wife of his at home, had frequently shown willingness to bestow themselves and occasionally their comfortable incomes on the light-hearted fellow who had neither a regular profession, ascertained means, nor (so it seemed) a local habitation. In fact he was a universal favourite with women, for no better reason than that he was always light-hearted, flatteringly ready to be at their beck and call, manly, a proficient in every kind of sport, and last, though not least, as fine and good-looking a specimen of manhood as existed in the United Kingdom.

The self-contained woman who lived in

21*

the secluded little cottage at Norwood, letting lodgings in order to be "no drag on poor Ted," and in order that he might have a place to go to when there were no good sporting country quarters open to him, had hard work at times to possess her soul in patience when she pictured him surrounded by attractive women. What chance had she, she would ask herself, in her plain dresses and house-care-worn air, against these smart society dames and demoiselles with their minds at peace and hearts at ease? His frank references to some of them and his outspoken admiration for them did not deceive her a bit. She knew that men can speak frankly and avow open admiration without turning a hair, even when far deeper feelings are in question than liking and admiration. She did not know that he habitually posed as a bachelor when he was away· from her, but she surmised that she was never on the *tapis*. Accordingly, jealousy claimed her for its tormenting own perpetually, and the fact of her not being able to put her finger on any individual object did not make its pangs a bit the easier to bear.

Before he had been twenty four hours at Trelyn, Ted Greg had thrown off and forgotten that he had experienced any feeling of embarrassment about the Poynters.

Ella came down the day after her accident looking very pale and pretty and rather inclined to appreciate Mr. St. Austle more than she had ever done. She saw that he closely watched both herself and Ted Greg when the latter was introduced to her,

and she attributed this display of interest
to a jealous dislike on Guy's part to seeing
another man approach her.   But neither
Ted Greg's appearance nor Ted Greg's
name held any personal interest for the
girl.   She greeted her new acquaintance
with such absolute unconcern that Guy
felt sure it was not on her step-daughter's
account that Mabel had shown emotion on
first hearing of and meeting this new figure
on the canvas.

That Mr. Greg would quickly ingratiate
himself with the whole party had been a
foregone conclusion in Sir Walter's mind,
when he gave the invitation to his old
chum!   But he had not been prepared to
see Ted concentrate most of the attention
of the whole party on himself, and become
the pivot on which the principal arrange-

ments of the day turned. The baronet had an airy way of his own, which was apt to lead people whithersoever he willed. But this was quite blown aside by Ted's stronger airiness, which held as great a charm for Walter as for the others.

Even Laura, happy, contented, and placidly proud as she was of her husband and her position, soon began to declare that the hunting days were too dull for endurance, and that the house was not like itself without Mr. Greg. While Mrs. Poynter cultivated him assiduously, and led him on to make innumerable small confidences to her about many things that were vital to him, such as likely colts that were being kept, and syndicates for the purchase of shares in divers railways, that were bound to pay a hundred and fifty per cent. within a couple of months at the latest. But confidential as he waxed on these matters—irritatingly confidential he seemed to Guy St. Austle—he never lifted the curtain that concealed his home or domestic life. This was Tom Tiddler's ground, and though Mabel skirmished round it, she had never ventured to put her foot upon it. Nevertheless, her determination to find out whether or not this man had a wife, either in the past or present, remained unaltered.

The deserted wife and children of Robert Davis, once millionaire and still missing man, were always very much to the fore at Trelyn Towers. They lived in one of the prettiest houses on St. Austle's property. They paid no rent, they were free of the Trelyn dairy, garden produce, poultry-

yard, and indeed of everything else that
belonged to Sir Walter St. Austle.

In one direction the latter had re-
trenched enormously since his marriage.
He had put down his training and breeding
establishments, sold his horses, and fore-
sworn all the seductive joys of the turf.
But in spite of his own impecuniosity and
Laura's plain, unvarnished pennilessness, he
had refused to curtail or economise at
Trelyn. In the stronghold of his old race
he would still play the open-handed part
which had been handed to him intact
through a long line of forbears. He was
made of the material that can face utter
ruin, but not mediocre meannesses. In
giving up the turf he had made his grand
sacrifice, and after that he resolutely
declined to do any more pinching and

screwing. While the St. Austles lived at Trelyn, they would always live like St. Austles. So when Laura told him that she "hated to see poor Anna, who had always had plenty of horses and carriages at her disposal, without even a pony-trap now," Sir Walter applauded his wife for the kindly thought, and presented Mrs. Davis with the prettiest little waggonette Bodmin could build, and the handsomest little upstanding cob that a well-known Cornish breeder could breed.

In his careless, forgetful way, Ted Greg had forgotten to associate Lady St. Austle with Robert Davis, the missing forger and bankrupt. Accordingly when, having been taken down to see Mrs. Davis, her pretty house and new acquisitions, he asked: "Where does her husband hang out? or is she a widow?" Laura felt herself constrained to tell him the whole story, though she was very much pained to do it.

"Poor chap! and you've never heard of him since?" he said, sympathetically. He was a sinner himself, this poor, too readily influenced Ted Greg, but he was very tolerant to the sins and faults and follies of others. He thought now far more of the suffering entailed upon Robert by his sin, than of the sin which had entailed the suffering. There was a very tender look in his eyes, as he referred to the erring man, and the erring man's sister liked him all the better for it.

"Awful ups and downs there are in the world!" he said feelingly; "the day your poor brother came to grief, a man settled himself into lodgings in a house I know in Norwood, in a very quiet kind of way. But he's a long-headed chap, and a lucky one into the bargain, and he's been awfully lucky in some speculations on the Stock Exchange, and has made a big pile, I fancy, from what he told me the other day. But he lives like a hermit in the midst of all his plenty."

"You live near him?—you seem to know him well?" Mrs. Poynter asked. She was always on the alert to pick up any facts that might help to reveal Ted Greg to her.

"Did I say I knew him well," he answered laughingly; "I mustn't sail under false colours, I only know him in the most casual way. We've smoked a few cigarettes together, and discussed the price

of stocks two or three times, but I know
no more of Denham than I did the first
day I saw him. The fact is, he's a 'cute
Yankee, and doesn't give himself away to
the first beggar for information."

"Do you know Norwood well, Mr
Greg?" Lady St. Austle put in; "do you
know Rezare; such a lovely place, I lived
there with my poor brother till I
married."

"Can't say I know Norwood well," he
said slowly, to the measured cadence of
the puffs at his cigarette. "I had a
sickening dose of the Crystal Palace in my
youth, so I keep out of eye-shot of it now
as much as possible. But now and again
I go down there and stay for a day or
two."

"Then perhaps you can recommend me

some lodging?" Mrs. Poynter said quickly. "Where you stay sometimes, for instance? Would they suit me for a week or two?"

He faced her with good-tempered defiance in his eyes.

"They wouldn't suit you at all," he said deliberately.

"Will you tell me where they are, and let me judge for myself?" she insisted, feeling that she was approaching Tom Tiddler's ground. "I should be a very easily-pleased lodger after a fastidious bachelor like you."

"I have never lodged in Norwood," he said cheerfully. "I stay there sometimes. The—friends with whom I stay have no lodgings to let, I assure you."

The upshot of this conversation was that Mr. Greg wrote to his wife at once, and one paragraph of his letter ran as follows :

"If any one comes sniffing round enquiring for lodgings before I come home, shut that person up and say you have none to let. In fact, I feel that it's *infra dig.* altogether that you should be taking lodgers. Remember, you did it without consulting me in Denham's case ; but I'll have no lady lodgers prying into your affairs and scenting out byegones that we both wish to bury."

"So there is a Mrs. Greg, ma'm," Mrs. Poynter's maid said that night when she was dressing her mistress for dinner. "Such a fine, handsome gentleman, and so much after the ladies as he is ! We none of us in the servants' hall thought of such a thing as his being married."

As a rule, Mrs. Poynter ruthlessly checked any little budding flowers of gossip from her maid, but now she felt too anxious to be dignified.

"How do you know there is a Mrs. Greg?" she asked.

"Mr. Greg came running down after the post-bag was locked, and gave a letter to James. I walked up to the post-office with James afterwards, and I happened to see it was addressed to Mrs. Greg, Glen Cottages, Norwood."

"Probably his mother," Mrs. Poynter said chillingly. But at the same time she resolved to find out a little more about the antecedents and present pursuits of the fascinating Ted, for it shocked her to see that a strong friendship seemed to be growing up between him and Ella.

"If what I fear is true, he ought to shun her, poor child!" she thought. Then the remembrance of an oath which her husband had made her take when he was dying came back upon her, and she was very uncomfortable, and very much inclined to confide all her troubles concerning Ted Greg to Guy. But the thought that if she did so the whole story would come out restrained her, for she feared Guy would not find that portion of it which related to herself pretty reading.

"I was an ass to write to Marian on St. Austle's note-paper," Ted Greg reflected, as soon as he had given his letter to James, "women are so d——d imprudent; she'll be writing to me here, and I shall get chaffed about my lady-correspondent.

Not that I want to keep her dark, the dear old girl, only as I haven't mentioned that I have a wife it will be awkward to do it now.   If it does come out, won't that Meredith girl give me beans."

CHAPTER IV.

THAT MEREDITH GIRL.

ONE of the most constant frequenters of the lake when the frost was at its hardest, of the hunting field, when the thaw set in, and of Trelyn Towers at all times, was a girl called May Meredith.

Under any circumstances she would have been an independent girl, both in spirit and action, but the conditions by which she had been surrounded from her cradle stage had fostered and developed the characteristic till it became abnormally out of proportion to her sex, some people said.

Well off, without being fabulously wealthy, fatherless and motherless from her child-

22*

hood, and absolutely her own mistress from the day she was twenty-one, she was now, at twenty-five, uncontrolled and uncontrollable.

She never did anything that even the censorious could take hold of as a wrong thing. All her instincts were generous and good, but they were rather of the broad, careless, masculine order than of the narrow, careful, feminine kind. She contended that at her age she was quite as competent to guide her own footsteps in the paths of honour and rectitude as any old, world-worn chaperone would be to guide them for her. Accordingly she lived at her pretty little place, Belhaven, on the banks of the Fal, with no other companion than her servants, horses and dogs.

Without being a bit of a beauty she was

a well-made girl of the stoutly-built, middle-height type. Her eyes were real blue, and were well set in a much bronzed, round, honest face. She rode and drove alone all over that part of the county, and on hunting-days she would often ask two or three men home to dine with her, thereby considerably scandalising many women who did much worse. But she never lured any young man on to suppose she would marry him if he asked her, or beguiled any married man into even seeming to swerve in his allegiance to his wife.

To this girl Ted Greg had seemed a unique and superior being. His good looks attracted her as no other man's had ever done, they were so bold and manly, and he seemed so utterly unconscious of them. With her customary disregard of mere appearances, she showed her liking for him fearlessly. And he responded to it.

The St. Austles favoured the intimacy, and agreed among themselves that " May might do much worse, and that it would be charming to have Ted Greg for a neighbour at Belhaven."

With uncalled-for discretion they said nothing of this hopeful plan of theirs to Mrs. Poynter, but Ella, who had become very intimate with Miss Meredith, was allowed to have an inkling of the truth, both from that young lady herself and from Lady St. Austle.

" I *do* like him better than any human being I ever saw before. I could bear to be ordered about by him, I believe," May admitted, and Lady St. Austle would say when May was not there :

" Ella, you must help me to give Mr. Greg chances with her. It would be such a good thing for him, poor fellow! for I'm sure he's not at all well off."

" I shouldn't care for a man twenty years older than myself, but as May Meredith seems to do it I hope she'll get him." It was easy to breathe this hope, for Ella did not want him herself. Accordingly she helped Lady St. Austle in a hundred ways to give Ted Greg " chances " of being alone with the independent young mistress of Belhaven.

He had begun by being attracted by the girl's hearty manner, love of horses, dogs, and sport, and a little, perhaps, by her obvious admiration for himself. She knew the country by heart, and was no trouble to him after the hounds, as she was better able

to give him a lead and show him the way
than he was to perform these offices for her.
Then he got familiar with and interested in
her couple of hunters, her blue roan cob,
and her yard full of hilarious noisy dogs.
It soon became his habit to saunter down
to Belhaven whenever he was not hunting
or shooting. He felt quite at home there.
May had no dislike to the smell of tobacco,
therefore she made no favour of letting him
smoke in her drawing-room. He inspected
her horses with an eye like a hawk's, until
the groom's life was a burden to him, and
the horses' coats were in better condition
than they had ever been before. He taught
her dogs tricks and obedience, alternately
commanding and caressing the intelligent
beasts until they, one and all, abjectly
worshipped him. And by the time he had

done these things he found that May was very much in love with him, and that the hours spent with her were the pleasantest he had known since——the days of his youth and folly.

He had no moral courage, and so when he found where they were drifting, he resigned himself to what he called "the inevitable," and made no effort to check their progress down the stream. It would be all right he told himself! In ten days, or a fortnight at the most, he would be going away; she wouldn't know his address, and as he wouldn't write to her there would be an end to it! In the meantime!—well it is needless to go into details concerning what went on in the meantime.

There was that subtle, perfect understanding between them, when each takes

the other entirely for granted, which many
a woman has had to rue, when it transpires
that the good faith of the "perfect understanding" has been on her side only.   May
was quite satisfied with things as they were
for a time.   Her handsome lover sought her
on every occasion.   His eyes were full of
love when they met hers, and he had a way
of holding her hand as if he hated to let it
go.   He was her own she felt as much as if
he had already asked her to be his wife, so
she showed him pretty plainly that she
loved him, and was supremely happy.

His well-poised head was not very strong
where women were concerned.   It was
flattering to him to feel that this girl
watched for his coming, and was weary at
his going.   He liked the authority she had
tacitly surrendered into his hands over her

stable and kennels. The thought of how pleasant it would be to be the master of this establishment, and of its bright-hearted mistress, would obtrude upon him far too often. Then the thought of Marian would intervene, checking and making him gloomy for a time in a way that was unaccountable to May. At these times he would swear to himself that he would go away the next day, or else tell May that he was married. But when the next day came, he neither went away, nor did he tell her, but just threw dull care aside, and enjoyed himself to the utmost.

The day before he wrote that letter to his wife—one passage from which has been given—Miss Meredith's horse had given her a nasty tumble at a bank by coming down on its knees and nose. She was not hurt, but a good deal shaken, and Ted Greg had been terribly frightened as he picked her up, and held her in a half-stunned state in his arms for a few minutes. By the time she recovered, the hounds, who were running fast at the time, were far away, and the field was out of sight.

"Oh, do go on, you'll be thrown out," she cried, and that she should think of him and of his pleasure first moved him strangely. He really loved her, and forgot everyone else for a moment, so touched was he by her consideration for himself.

"My darling, you don't suppose I am going on to leave *you*, do you?" he said tenderly, and as he spoke he bent his head down and kissed her.

It was the first time, and the girl had given him her whole heart, believing herself fully justified in doing so. There was no shame to her in the caress, but, on the contrary, much glory. That kiss seemed to her to bind them together and make them indissolubly one.

"My darling Ted! my own darling Ted!" she said, as he put her up on her horse. As she settled herself to her saddle she bent down and pressed her lips on to his forehead, and the consciousness that he had gone too far, sent the blood up into his face in a dark flush.

"We've lost the hounds hopelessly," she said, quite gaily for such a keen young sportswoman; "let us ride home and have some luncheon, and in the afternoon we'll look at that brown horse my man was saying yesterday would suit *you*. If it does I should like——"

She drew nearer to him, laid her hand on his arm, with a wealth of love and trust in her eyes, and went on:

"To give it to you, Ted!"

It was impossible for him to explain matters just now. She was nervous and shaken from the effects of her fall still. It would be cruel to deal her a blow now.

So, as to refuse the horse would be to make an explanation needful, and as explanations were things he always deferred making until they were dragged out of him, he lifted her hand to his lips and called her his "darling" again. He shrank from giving her pain while he was present to see it, and he put the thought of what she must suffer by-and-by away from him till a more convenient season.

They went back to Belhaven and

lunched, and he walked about afterwards
and exercised the authority she was thrust-
ing into his hands in a way that made
the groom and gardener hate him as
the coming master.

She had quite grasped by this time that
he was a poor man, and her generous
nature made her long to endow him with
all the things she felt he ought to have.
When it came to the point he could not
bring himself to refuse the brown hunter,
so she gave it to him, and it was arranged
that the horse should stand in her stables
until Ted left Trelyn, and could take it
away with him.

He was very fond of horses, and was
rapturously grateful to her for giving him
one. He knew that he would not be able
to afford to keep it, but that was a disagree-

able question which he felt he needn't consider yet, not for a week or two at any rate. He wished that she hadn't tempted him to take it, but his refusal would have hurt her, and he couldn't bear the idea of hurting a girl who was so evidently fond of him.

She gave him a ring before he left that day, a ring that had belonged to her father, a pigeon's-blood ruby that was worth a small fortune. It bothered him a little to think how he should account to Marian for the possession of this ring. But that, too, was a difficulty that would not be met just yet. So he let May slip the ring on his finger, and he wore it.

When he left her that day May wandered about in a state of happy excitement from room to room: Presently, in the depths of an easy chair in which he had been sitting, she saw an envelope. Picking it up she read the address :

" Edward Greg, Esq.,

" 2, Glen Cottages, Norwood, Surrey."

There was a letter in it, therefore she had an excuse for writing him a few lines and enclosing what she had found, " As it might be of importance," she said. She did not copy the address, there was no need for that, it was engraved on her memory.

Her messenger came back with a few lines of acknowledgment, beginning " My own darling," and subscribing himself, " Yours devotedly," but he did not sign his name, and she felt chilled.

In the course of a few days he had a letter from his wife. A letter in which she poured out all the pent-up passion of her heart. A letter reminding him of their early love, and of how it behoved them above all people to be all in all to one another. A letter that revealed the writer in every line as a loving, patient, proud, heart-sore woman, who would rather die than lose his love. A letter that touched Mr. Ted Greg considerably, and nearly brought the tears to his eyes, but that had not the power of keeping him away from unsuspicious May Meredith.

She met him now quite as if he were her avowed lover, rushing to meet him, holding out both hands and yielding up her lips frankly to his kisses.

"Have you told the St. Austles yet?"

she asked him, and he answered hesitatingly :

"They know I'm awfully fond of you ; I don't see that there is any need to tell them more. We're very happy as we are, aren't we, my darling ? "

" *That* we are !" she assented with energy. "Ted," she went on, "will you be as fond of this dear old place as I am ? "

" I love Belhaven !" he declared.

"That's right, and I love Belhaven better than ever because you do. I can't think how I shall get on here when you go away for a little time. Why must you go at all, Ted ? "

" I have heaps of business to attend to, but I'll soon come back," he promised recklessly, and then he changed the subject

23*

and tried to forget that he had got himself into a most frightful coil.

There were times when Ella Poynter felt sickeningly jealous of her friend May's happiness and the apparent prosperity of her love-affair. In spite of all the delicate encouragement she gave him, Guy St. Austle remained persistently cool to her, and devoted to her step-mother. If she could once detach him from the widow, she (Ella) felt sure she could catch him in the rebound.

At last chance—she thought it was Providence—favoured her.

They were speaking one night of the way in which handwriting revealed character, and as is usual when such discussions arise, some of the party were sceptical, while others believed firmly in the revelations as if they were Gospel truths. Guy, who was somewhat of an expert at the game, and who happened to know pretty nearly all that there was to be known about everyone present (with the exception of Ted Greg), had made some remarkably happy hits, and covered himself with glory. Suddenly Ella saw that Mr. Greg had not submitted himself to the ordeal.

"Won't you give Mr. St. Austle a scrap of your writing?" she asked, and then she went on; "we all know you pretty well, I think, Mr. Greg, and what we know is so nice that we want to know more."

"A scrap of my writing! certainly! but 1 mustn't write with intention, must I? and I'm afraid I haven't a bit written in blissful ignorance that I was going to be judged by it anywhere," he answered, and May Meredith put in quickly :

"I have a note of yours in my pocket, Ted, that will do."

She pulled it out forthwith, looked at it, blushed and laughed, tore off the beginning and ending, leaving only a few uncompromising words that related to the horses and dogs.

It was handed to Ella to pass on to Guy St. Austle, and as she glanced at it she changed colour and looked across, half vindictively, half triumphantly, at her stepmother.

"Come Ella ! look sharp," May Meredith said, impatiently, "I'm longing to know if Mr. St. Austle will find out anything fresh about Ted."

"Your writing is very familiar to me,"

Ella said incisively, looking from Mrs. Poynter to Ted Greg, "I know it by heart, for I have a letter of yours——"

"Ella!" Mrs. Poynter had risen and come round to the excited girl's side, "My dear child! stop," she whispered in an agony of pathetic appeal.

"You have a letter of Mr. Greg's!" May Meredith put in haughtily.

"Yes—and I'll show it too," said the little fury.

CHAPTER V,

" You deciphered Mr. Greg's character from his writing pretty accurately, now will you decipher the character of the man who wrote *this?* "

Ella Poynter was the speaker, and of course the person she addressed was Mr. St. Austle. She held a letter out to him as she spoke, and before he gave himself time to think he read :

" ' My own only darling—bravest as well as dearest of women—if I ever forget what you——' "

" It's Greg's writing! where on earth did you get this letter ? "

"It's the letter I wanted to show you before—the one I found among my father's papers; it *is* Mr. Greg's writing, isn't it?"

She spoke eagerly, with flushed cheeks and sparkling eyes. At last his eyes would be opened to the unworthiness of her step-mother.

"I am not sure that it is," he said coldly, handing her back the letter as he spoke; "it was not fair of you, Miss Poynter, to trick me into reading a letter I have already refused to look at."

Tears of vexation sprang into her eyes.

"How blindly infatuated you must be," she panted out; "I tell you this letter was marked in my father's writing, 'From my false wife's lover,' yet you're ready to take that man's ——"

"Hush!" he said sternly, and Ella was

startled into silence as she followed the direction of his eyes, and saw Mrs. Poynter herself coming towards them.

"What has agitated you so, Ella?" she asked nervously. She had no suspicion of what the matter under discussion between Guy and Ella had been, but the appearance of an intimate understanding and of confidential intercourse between them was distressing to the woman to whom Guy had vowed fidelity.

"Shall I tell her?" Ella asked maliciously.

"Certainly not!" Mr. St. Austle said hastily; then seeing that Mrs. Poynter looked hurt and mystified, he added:

"Miss Poynter has been allowing her imagination to run away with her; unless she curbs it she will get into mischief I'm afraid."

"How *can you* speak of me in that way?" Ella whispered, subdued but frantically jealous still; but Guy instead of responding to her followed Mabel to the window recess in which she had settled herself.

"Don't be annoyed with me," he pleaded, in such a low tone that though she strained her ears to the utmost Ella could not catch a word.

"I'm not annoyed, only puzzled," Mrs. Poynter rejoined.

"Not more puzzled than I am myself; come into the garden and have a turn," he added, pushing open the window, and to Ella's chagrin Mrs. Poynter obeyed him at once, though she had nothing but her indoor gear on.

"Flattering him by doing exactly whatever he chooses to ask her, even at the risk of getting rheumatism in her old head," the girl thought indignantly as the pair who were outraging her passed out of her sight. The next moment she ran after them, calling out:

"Shall I fetch you a wrap, Mrs. Poynter? You have always told me you could never stand the frosty air, even when you were young."

"Thanks, Ella, I shall be very glad of the wrap; my poor old head is giving premonitory symptoms of neuralgia already."

The offer was accepted in such perfect good faith, Mrs. Poynter was so absolutely unconscious of there being anything to be ashamed of in the fact of her being no longer a young woman, that Ella retired discomfited, and did not reappear with the wrap which she had so considerately offered, but neither of them noticed her non-appearance.

"And now," said Mrs. Poynter, when they found themselves alone in a sheltered, high laurel-hedged walk, "will you tell me what the mystery is which Ella and you are trying to manufacture?"

She spoke very lightly, and as if the matter in question were of no moment whatever to her, but she became grave enough when Guy replied:

"It is about Greg; for some reason or other Ella has become suspicious of him."

"Good heavens, *why?*" Mrs. Poynter cried; "how I wish he had never come here; how is it possible that any suspicion of him should have been created in her mind?"

" Then there is some ground——" he was beginning, when Mabel interrupted him.

" Yes, yes, at least I fear—I hardly know what I fear. I only wish the poor child had never seen or even heard of the man. It's the very irony of fate that she should have done so after all the precautions that have been taken."

She spoke more to herself than to him, but he answered her :

" You're not afraid that he has interested her seriously, are you? If so, I can assure you your alarms are groundless. She has been well pleased to see him devoted to her friend May Meredith, and has only liked him herself in a casual, friendly sort of way that meant nothing at all up to the present time. Now she dislikes him ; can *you* tell me why ? "

He watched her keenly, and she felt that he did so, but there was neither fear nor shame in her sweet eyes as she lifted them to his.

"It must be intuition," she said, "some day I may tell you why poor Ella has taken this instinctive dislike to him, but not now; I dare not tell you now."

"It can't be anything that concerns herself, thank God for that!" he thought, and then he led her on to identify herself with his dramatic and literary interests, without asking for any expression of more directly personal feeling from her for the time.

"Will you have the courage to witness my possible failure the first night my play comes out in my company?" he asked, and she told him:

"It will be a triumph I feel sure, and I

shall be proud to be with you to be the first to congratulate you."

"Thank you, Mabel," he said, and then he tucked her hand into his arm, and though not a word of love was spoken between them they each felt that they were being drawn across the invisible barrier which had separated them.

When they went in to luncheon that day they found Mrs. Davis seated at the table brimming over with excitement and emotion. At last, as she had always prophesied, she had heard from the lost Robert. He had written "most affectionately and sensibly," she told them, and had sent her bank notes for a hundred pounds. How he had got hold of her address passed all understanding ; his having done so "proved conclusively," she declared, "how vigilantly he must have sought for tidings of her." The one drawback to her current contentment was that he gave her no hint as to his own whereabouts. There was no address, and the letter had been posted at the General Post Office, so she had not the faintest clue to his local habitation. But sufficient for the faithful woman's day was the hearing from him and the hundred pounds.

*　　　*　　　*　　　*

Up in that quiet little cottage in the most secretive part of Norwood the tide of life ebbed and flowed very gently and monotonously. Sometimes for days together Mrs. Greg would see nothing of her strange lodger, who would depart at night with a small Gladstone, and reappear after a brief absence at night again, always much muffled up about the head and throat as though he feared the inclemencies of the climate to which he avowed he could never get accustomed. Then again he would have a long spell of home staying, and while these spells were on him he would make little overtures of a friendly nature towards Mrs. Greg when she came in to superintend the arrangement of the table for his eight-o'clock dinner.

On one of these occasions she told him that her husband was staying at Trelyn Towers, in Cornwall, with an old friend of his, Sir Walter St. Austle, and to her surprise Mr. Denham betrayed unwonted interest and animation at hearing of a fact which to her belief could not concern him in the slightest degree.

He knew that it was a dangerous topic

for him to venture upon, still he could not resist the fascination of skirmishing round it, and trying to gain some tidings of those who were dearer to him than anything else in this world, excepting his love of speculation and his longing for security.

"Sir Walter St. Austle married the sister of a man who was well-known in the mercantile world, didn't he?" Mr. Denham asked, and Mrs. Greg told him she "had but a dim recollection of the affair, but she fancied there had been some commercial scandal connected with the St. Austle marriage."

"To be sure; it happened about the time I came here, if I remember rightly," Denham went on, and Mrs. Greg, who was arranging flowers on the table at the moment, did not observe the half-scared,

24*

half-sly, expression of his face as he added:
"The man who came to grief left a wife
and children, if I remember?—let me
see, did the man die? or did he cut and
run?"

"I forget," Mrs. Greg said carelessly,
"but my husband will be home in a few
days, and he will be able to tell you all
about them. Oh, by the way, he does say
in a letter I had from him to-day that ' that
scoundrel Davis's wife and children are
living in one of St. Austle's houses at
Trelyn, and the good fellow supports them
entirely.' Perhaps Davis was the man you
mean?"

"Yes, Davis was the name," Mr. Denham
assented. Then suddenly he became very
thoughtful, and Mrs. Greg, who was used
to his moods, went away softly, leaving him

alone with his dainty dinner and doleful reflections.

It was this information which enabled him to send the bank-notes for a hundred pounds to his wife, together with the promise that a like sum should be sent to her every four months until such time as the enterprise in which he had embarked should prove successful enough to enable him to reclaim his beloved wife and children.

He forgot in his egotism and uxoriousness to say anything about the sister whom he had defrauded and the brother-in-law whom he had duped. His wife in her balmy satisfaction at hearing from him at all, and at having her needs partially supplied by him again, was quite regardless of this carelessness or callousness, whichever it might have been. But Laura felt hurt at it, and her husband resentful about it, so resentful that for the first time since the disaster he permitted himself to say some truthfully hard things about Robert Davis.

"He's a rogue right through," Walter St. Austle said to his friend Ted Greg; "he robbed his own sister and duped me, and if I can ever help to get him out of the country for the country's good I'll do it. That poor woman, his wife, and his children, are better off without him than they ever would be with him. He's my wife's brother, but for his own sake it's to be hoped he'll never give me the chance of helping justice to handle him."

"Is he handsome—like Lady St. Austle?" Ted Greg asked for the sake of saying something about a matter that was profoundly uninteresting to him, and yet about which he was expected to speak.

"Not a bit! You'll find a photograph of him kicking about in my wife's album. I won't have him framed and glazed and put into prominent places with the rest of the family, but poor Laura, who can never be got to see that he is nothing better than a common swindler, has a grateful recollection of the scoundrel and keeps his likeness in her book. I'll show it to you to-night."

Sir Walter did show it to Mr. Greg that night, and the smug mutton-chop-whiskered face struck Ted Greg with a curious sense of familiarity. But he could not locate it, or remember whether it belonged to his childhood or to his later years.

*   *   *   *   *

The Trelyn party had broken up and gone their several ways. To the annoyance of Sir Walter and Lady St. Austle, and to the inwardly heart-broken chagrin of May Meredith, Ted Greg had gone without speaking those decisive words which he had led the girl to suppose he would speak. Bitterly she blamed him, and not less bitterly did she blame herself for having given the St. Austles the right to enquire whether the open and unabashed love-making which had taken place in their house had come to a legitimate conclusion or not. But her anger against her tardy lover was always short-lived, and was invariably succeeded by an even warmer thrill of love for him and longing for his presence than had gone before.

For several days after his departure,

May Meredith possessed her soul in patience in the vain hope and expectation that the next post would bring a letter from him, but no letter came, and when a full week had elapsed she could be patient no longer. She determined that she would write to him! She had the right to do this! She " belonged to a class with whom no gentleman would dare to tamper and trifle," she told herself proudly. The words of love that he had addressed to her were such words as no man living . *could* have addressed to *her* unless he looked upon her as his future wife. It was only that he was negligent and procrastinating; she had always recognised these qualities in him. Or perhaps he was ill and unable to write? The bare idea of this being the case melted away the last bit of her pride and reticence, and caused her to sit down and pour out her heart upon paper, after an injudicious woman's most injudicious manner.

How heartily she congratulated herself in her weakness and blindness, poor girl, on having got hold of his address. Of course "he would have given it to her if she had asked him for it," she told herself; "probably he thought he had given it to her, and all this time he might be waiting expectantly for a few lines from her?" He should not wait much longer. He should soon know how absolutely devoted she was to him, how she trusted him, and how proudly glad she would be to share that good fortune and dear home, which were hers to do as she liked with, with him.

The rebound from the restraint she had exercised over herself for a week was such a strong one, that it broke down all those slight barriers of reserve which she would have respected under a more normal condition of affairs. If she had not been tortured by doubt and distrust of him into the reactionary state of ultra-generosity of feeling towards him, she would have worded her letter more circumspectly. As it was she wrote :

"My own darling Ted

"Your silence has made me horribly anxious ! Something must I fancy have happened to make you forgetful—or at least neglectful—of me for a week. Walter St. Austle tells me he has had a few lines from you, 'written in good spirits,' he says, so I comfort myself by thinking that at least you are not ill. But, oh Ted ! how can you write in good spirits when you're away from me and must know that I am wearing my heart out with impatience to see you again. The place misses you I'm sure, for even the rooms look sad now you're gone. The horses and dogs miss you, and I *more* than miss you, my own love. The May Meredith of three months ago would have laughed to scorn the May Meredith who is writing this. But let those laugh who win, and the May Meredith who writes this has won what she considers the greatest prize on earth, and that is your love, for I *have* won it, haven't I, my own darling Ted?

"How glad I am that I never frittered even a little bit of my heart away on any other man before you came. Are you glad too?

"I can't help telling you all I feel, for I owe it to you that I feel so strongly.

"Don't wait for a post; wire a reply to this that will set my uneasiness at rest.   The words I hope the telegram will contain are, 'Well, and coming.'

"Yours always and entirely,

"MAY."

Ted Greg had been at home with his wife for several days when this letter was delivered at the cottage.   His habits even when in that humble home were those of a sybarite compared to those in which Mrs Greg found it possible to indulge.   The one servant was quite unable to supply all the service and attention which was demanded by her master, consequently his wife had to supplement the maid-of-all-work's efforts. It was Mabel who 'arranged' the hot bath he liked to take before dinner in the evening, and his morning's cold tub. These things together with their accompaniments of cork mat and bath towels, were always ready for him when he wanted them, and so it never occurred to him to enquire who carried up the heavy cans of water from the basement. If he had seen Marian doing it he would have asked her " why the devil she didn't make her slavey do it ? " and would have been ruffled at the spectacle of his wife doing hard manual labour for his sake for a few minutes. But as he did not see her, he closed his mind against the entrance of all speculation on the subject, and went on enjoying his bath in an unruffled mood.

On the morning that May's letter was

delivered at the cottage, he was enjoying an early cup of coffee in bed when the postman came. It was so unusual for him to have letters addressed to him here that his wife took it up to him at once, and expressed some faint curiosity as to "who his lady correspondent could be?" The conditions of her life had made her sensitively jealous and suspicious, and though she battled against these demons ·to the best of her ability they over-mastered her at times.

A dark flush covered his face as he recognised the writing of the girl he had so cruelly befooled. But his manner was un-embarrassed and his tone unconcerned as he said :

"It's from Lady St. Austle, I suppose, she does a lot of note-writing for St. Austle."

He flung himself back upon the pillows as he spoke, opening the letter and holding his hands in such a way that she could not get a glimpse of its contents. In a moment he crumpled it up, and turned round sleepily.

" Only a beast of a bill after all," he said, and Marian turned away impatiently, for she knew he was lying to her.

An hour afterwards, having carefully and fastidiously tubbed, dressed and breakfasted, he went off to Town, and Mrs. Greg went up to make the bed and put the room to rights. The first thing her eyes lighted upon was the crumpled letter thrown carelessly on the dressing-table. Conquering her scruples about invading his privacy for once, she picked it up, smoothed it out and read it.

CHAPTER VI.

WHEN Ted Greg read that letter from May
Meredith he felt as much shocked as a careless, selfish man can feel, when he first tastes
the bitterness of the fruit he has planted
and cherished. That May was thoroughly
and seriously in earnest he had known uneasily for some time. But he had mistakenly
reckoned on her pride preserving her from
pursuing him for an explanation, when he
had retreated without having given her
one. He had failed to bear in mind that a
woman in love has a habit of putting her
pride in her pocket, where the man she is in
love with is concerned.

To do him full justice he felt very much ashamed of himself, and very desirous of keeping the cause of that feeling of shame a secret from Miss Meredith still.

"By Jove! if she ever finds out that I'm a married man she'll turn and rend me, round on me to Marian, and then there'll be the devil to pay," he told himself as he read the warmly-worded epistle for the second time. "I suppose I must answer it?" he thought ruefully, "but how?— that's the question." Then he came to the conclusion that there was no hurry for a day or two, he would think it over. The sense of relief which he experienced on coming to this decision made him careless, and the effect of this carelessness was that the tell-tale letter was reposing on the dressing-table when Marian went up to arrange the room, with the scrupulous cleanliness and dainty care, which he always expected should be maintained in the little establishment.

Fortunately there was no one by to see the paroxysm of rage and pain which possessed her, as she read the words which proved how false the man had been for whom she had sacrificed everything that a woman holds dear. Foully false to her, and cruelly false to the other woman, who evidently wrote in the belief that she was justified in the tone she adopted towards him.

"He is tired of me," the miserable woman moaned, falling on her knees by the side of the bed; "tired of me, of *me*, who still worship him as much as on that unhappy day when he first told me he loved me. He

25*

has been ashamed of me for a long time; I know it now, though I have shut my eyes to it for so long. And now he has taught another woman to love him to her misery, and *how* he must have seemed to love her, for her to write in this way."

The words, " Whatever *is* the matter, ma'am," spoken in a spasm of curiosity and astonishment by her young servant girl, roused Mrs. Greg to a recollection of what was due to appearances and herself.

" The matter! oh! nothing," she said, hastily rising up and clutching that crimi- nating letter closely in her hand. Was it Ted's honour she wanted to spare by the concealment? or was it the desire to save herself from mortification? Who can tell? Her motives were mixed, as merely human motives must always be.

The whole of that day she wasted in vain repining and idle tears. She was not made of the stern stuff that can cast an idol out of the heart when the idol totters unworthily. It hurt her horribly to think that the man she had loved, to her sorrow, should have used blandishments and endearments towards another woman. But she could not dislike the man, she could only hate the woman who had beguiled him.

For, of course, she argued that this May must have tempted him in an unseemly and disgraceful manner before he could so grossly have forgotten himself, as to make the serious love to her which May's letter implied he had made. How could she punish the bold girl without bringing odium on Ted? Faulty as he was his wife would not be the one to hurt him in the eyes of the world. But the bold woman who was pursuing him with her amorous written words into the sanctuary of his home should be made to feel the full force of her indiscretion.

How could she be got at? that was the question. She had given neither address nor surname. She had merely signed herself "his always and entirely, May." For all Mrs. Greg knew it might be a married woman, who was striving to take Ted away from her. There was more bitterness in this possibility than in the idea of its being an unmarried girl who was her rival. A married woman, she knew from sad experience, would be more likely to forfeit her position for the sake of retaining him than an unmarried one would be.

"If I could only get at her I'd stab her to the heart as she has stabbed me," the unhappy woman thought; "I'd send this letter to her husband, and wring a promise from Ted never to see or speak to her again on pain of my exposing her." Then she raged afresh at her own inability to get hold of this hateful May, and finally came to the conclusion that the only thing she could do was to tax Ted outright with his perfidy, and make his full confession the price of her silence.

He came home in quite a cheerful mood that night. His conscience had ceased to prick him with regard to May; indeed he had almost forgotten the circumstance of having had a letter from her, and was entirely oblivious of the fact of having lost it. Some shares in a syndicate, in which he had recently invested, had been sold advantageously, and he was altogether feeling prosperous and happy. On this lively mood of his Marian's depression fell like cold water, and it was in both an injured and angry tone that he enquired, " What the devil is the matter with you ? "

" This ! " she gasped out, passion overcoming her at sight of his nonchalance, and as she spoke she held the letter out open before him.

He caught it from her, and tore it to tatters in a moment, muttering as he did so that it served her right for prying into his correspondence.

" I can explain everything if you'll only leave off foaming and fulminating, Marian," he went on after a few moments.

" Who is the woman ? give me her name,

tell me where she lives and I will write her such a letter as will teach her not to address another woman's husband as her 'own darling Ted' again."

"Let the poor girl alone, Marian; she's innocent of all wrong-doing. She has got fond of me, believing me to be an unmarried man."

"Is *she* a married woman?"

"No, she's a girl, I tell you, and a very nice girl too; but even if it had been a married woman you, of all people, might have judged her leniently."

"You coward!" she flamed out, "you taunt me with the folly and sin you taught me to commit. Oh, Ted! forgive me" (he had turned away with an oath), "I am half mad at the idea of your thinking of another woman. Tell me that it was not your fault; tell me that she led you on, tell me you have not been deliberately false to me?"

"I tell you the girl's as good a girl as ever stepped; we got friendly and she mistook my friendliness for a deeper feeling, that's the long and the short of it. When I found she expected me to propose I hadn't the heart or the moral courage to undeceive her. So you see, Marian, if anyone is to be blamed for it, you must blame me, but I don't see that you have any reason to complain or to find fault about such a trifle."

"No reason to complain when you have led a girl on to address you in such passionate language? What do you think I am made of, Ted? God knows all pride has been long since crushed down in me, but it is not quite extinct, and to my sorrow I have the power of loving and being jealous as strongly developed in me as ever."

"There's where you're so silly" he said, turning away from the unpleasant spectacle of her flushed, tear-stained face, "you're my wife, and even if I wanted to chuck you I couldn't do it, we're too tightly tied up for that, for I believe you're too fond of me to divorce me even if I gave you good cause for doing it, which I shan't do."

He laughed airily as he concluded his argument. In a way he was fond of his wife, and in a way he liked May Meredith. But the reflection that his conduct had already caused exquisite pain to Marian, and would smite May even more cruelly when she came to know of it, caused him only the most transitory feeling of regret.

"It was awkward," he admitted, "annoying, in fact that, May should have been such a little fool as to pour her heart out on paper. Women of the nineteenth century, with ages of experience behind them, ought at least to have learnt that no more fatal folly than this lavish letter-writing can be committed." As for his wife, he hoped it would be a lesson to her not to pry into his correspondence again. At her age she ought to have done with jealousy and every other dramatic folly and settle down into a nice, lady-like endurance of the present and course of preparation for the future. For in spite of his own lack of either religious feeling or profession, he liked the idea of his wife being bound by scruples of faith and morality now that she was his wife. A woman with no regard for both these things was certain eventually to go very much to the bad, therefore it was incumbent on Mrs. Greg to conceive and carry out a high-toned life in which unquestioning devotion and absolute fidelity to himself in thought, word, and deed was the first condition. He was quite easy in his conscience about leaving her unwritten to for several weeks while he was enjoying the society of people who were either unconscious or forgetful of Marian's existence. But he would have considered her conduct unwomanly, un-wife-like, and altogether unworthy, if, when he came home, she had given him a cool welcome, or he had discovered that she had given either words or smiles of more than the most ordinary civility to any other man.

As a rule, he had been able to exorcise the torturing demons of jealousy which occasionally took possession of her. His way was winning even if it was careless, and he had the great hold on her affection of never worrying or finding fault in an irritable manner about trifles. If things displeased him he frankly rapped out a condemnatory oath, but he neither harped upon the unpleasant subject, nor recurred to it when she had done her best to rectify the fault. In addition, he was open-handed. When he had money he gave it to her freely and did not suspiciously cross-examine her as to what she had done with it. She was also still absurdly proud of his appearance. The charms of his fine figure, swagger manner, and handsome, manly face were as potent with her as ever.

So, in consequence of these traits and appearances, she remained his romantically willing slave still, and the woman who was reserved and haughty with all the rest of the world was as humble and pliant in her dealings with him as the veriest Sultan could desire.

But on this occasion she was not readily appeased and the demon of jealousy was not easily exorcised. When he turned away from her with an airy explanation that was half a rebuke, she did not follow him with a prompt offer to make it up, forget the offence and say no more about it. On the contrary she followed him with a request that at least he would write a letter to the young lady who had addressed him in the apparent belief that she was addressing her future husband at her (Marian's) dictation and give it to her to post.

"If you won't do me this poor justice, this small favour, I will leave you to-day and you shall never be troubled by the sight or hearing of me again. I mean it, Ted! You know when I make up my mind to a course I take it," she said firmly, and he began to feel that he was liable to being forced into an unpleasant position by her determination.

"You're the most unreasonable woman that ever stepped," he said, with a fair show of indignation. "I tell you I'll put an end to it, and never see or speak to the girl again ; but I am not going to give her up to your claws. Women are so apt to develop the tigress when they're scratched slightly. You would dictate a good many cruel and a good many unjust words, my dear, and I don't mean to be the one to write them."

" Then I shall leave you to-night," she said quietly.

" You'll not be fool enough — I mean unkind enough to do anything of the kind when you're a little cooler, Marian," he replied, trying a move that had never failed to checkmate her before, namely, holding out his face towards hers for a kiss.

She shook her head vehemently, and blushed deeply.

" You evidently bestow such caresses too freely for me to value them any longer, Ted—at least, not until I have some assurance that for the future you will not dis- honour yourself and wrong me by bestowing them on anybody else. Once more!—will you give me this assurance in the way I ask you about this person 'May,' at least ?"

"For Heaven's sake, don't speak so contemptuously about a girl who's simply a perfect girl, and who belongs to one of the best families in the county."

"I've no wish to speak contemptuously of the girl; poor girl! I pity her too much for being your victim to the extent of thinking that you mean to marry her. But I can only speak of her by the name she signs to that very unguarded epistle. Poor girl! how she would smart if she knew that you threw it about carelessly for any other woman to pick up and read!"

" I was so bothered and shocked at her

writing to me that I hardly knew what I was doing this morning," he said self-excusingly. " You see, Marian, I never asked her to write to me even, never dreamt of giving her my address——"

" She loved you and found it out. I love you, and will find hers out yet," Marian interrupted. Then she left him, and he knew presently by the sounds that came from the room above that she was packing her trunks and preparing to carry out her threat of leaving him.

A wave of the old tender feeling for her, which had grown faint and weak of late years, swept over his soul as he thought of what his home, seldom as he inhabited it, would be without her. This was accompanied by the sharp, stinging recollection of all he had led her to lose in the bygone

26*

time when she was a young beauty, the mistress of a lovely home, the mother of a much-loved child!

"By Jove! I owe it to her to satisfy her, and make an end of it with May at once," he cried impulsively, as he seated himself at her davenport and wrote:

"I take the whole blame of what has unfortunately occurred on myself. Your letter has been inadvertently opened and read by my wife. I can only humbly apologise to you for not having told you I was a married man, but the subject never seemed to come on the *tapis* naturally, and I most blamably shrank from introducing it. I need not assure you that I shall always entertain the most profound respect for you, and that my wife exonerates you from all blame in this unfortunate misconception. With the deepest humility and regret, allow me to subscribe myself, yours most sincerely,

"Edward Greg."

It was a bitter pill to swallow having to write this letter, but his spirits rose slightly as he reflected that, at any rate, it would appease Marian and make things all straight with her again. However, when he took it up and showed it to her, with many affectionate protestations of his desire to "please her and set her heart at rest at any cost to the young lady," she astonished him by saying, "If that is really your desire, Ted, you will now address this letter and give it to me to post!"

"That will give you the command of her

name and address, Marian ; that would be beastly unfair——" he began hotly ; but when she turned away with a short, angry sigh and recommenced her packing, he gave in to the extent of saying :

"Come to the post-office with me and see me drop it into the box, will *that* satisfy you ? "

" Yes," she agreed, and he ran downstairs and was standing smoking his cigarette with the letter in its envelope, and the latter sealed, stamped, and addressed in his hand.

But at the last his heart had failed him, and for the letter he had submitted to his wife for her approval he had substituted his card, with the name of his club printed on it, and the words :

" Write to club if you don't hear from me in a week or two.—Yours, TED."

" That will choke her off without telling her the whole brutal truth," he thought complacently. He had no intention of writing to her in a week or ever again, and he relied on pique and pride keeping her silent. He did not know May Meredith!

CHAPTER VII.

"I AM YOUR MOTHER."

MRS. POYNTER and Ella had been home about three weeks, and to the growing jealous distress of the girl it was clear that a happy understanding had been arrived at between her step-mother and Mr. St. Austle. Mrs. Poynter looked so gently and he so triumphantly happy that there could be no doubt about it, and so Ella was only angry and not astonished when Mrs. Poynter said :

"You have often heard me say I should never marry again, Ella ; well, dear, I have thought better of that resolution, and I am going to marry Guy St. Austle. Your home will be with me still, dear, till you leave it for a happier one of your own."

Mrs. Poynter's own happiness had made her feel more kindly and speak more affectionately to her step-daughter than she had done since the discovery of the attempted interference on Ella's part while they were at Trelyn. The woman had intuitively felt that the girl's hand was against her with regard to Guy. But now the girl's hand had been proved powerless. Guy had been more ardent than ever in his determination to overcome her unworded motive for refusing him. And now that he had overcome it, and she was openly and legitimately engaged to him, she allowed the happiness that was in her heart to expand fully and freely, and overflow upon all within her radius.

But Ella's way of receiving and responding to her avowal was chilling.

"Any home of my own would be happier than one with you has ever been, and as for staying on as a visitor in a house where Mr. St. Austle was master I'd rather go out as a scullery-maid than do it."

An inkling of the truth concerning Ella's sentiments for Guy had already made its way into Mabel Poynter's mind. However, she tried to oust it as often as it became obtrusive. In reply to Ella's pettish speech she said temperately :

"My dear child, if you would only believe that I wish to make you happy you wouldn't set yourself against me in this blindfold way. And as for Mr. St. Austle, you liked him very much at first, and he will be such a real friend to you, Ella, if you'll let him."

"I hate him now," Ella gasped out furiously. She knew that her anger against him was unfounded and unreasonable; but!—she had permitted herself to fall in love with him without sufficient cause, and as he had not returned it she now fancied she hated him, and cultivated her fancy with undue ferocity.

"I hate him, and I suppose you won't be such a tyrant as to keep me here against my will to see and be sickened by the love-making and the wedding preparations. I shall write to May Meredith, and ask her to have me for a time; she has asked me to pay her a visit, and I shall do it now."

There was nothing to be said against

this proposition. Mrs. Poynter liked May Meredith in spite of the latter's infatuation for Mr. Greg. But the Greg episode was passed, and its consequences over she believed, so there would be no fear of Ella's meeting him at Belhaven.

It turned out, however, that May Meredith could not receive Ella at Belhaven just then. "I am coming up to town on business that is important to myself; perhaps you will be able to help me about it. When it's over, *one way or another*, you shall come back to Belhaven with me, and stay as long as you like, dear."

With this bit of hope deferred Ella had to possess her soul in patience, and remain on in her step-mother's house, a silent and disgusted spectator of Guy St. Austle's attentions to his future wife, even though she could not complain of any undue love-making.

A fortnight passed, and then Ella had a telegram from Miss Meredith, saying:

" Call on me to-morrow, any time, at the Great Western Hotel."

Appearances and locality were held in high account by Miss Poynter. It annoyed her that she could not tell her girl-friends that she was going either to the Métropole or the Grand to see, and probably stay with, her *great* friend, Miss Meredith, a Cornish heiress. It sounded humdrum to say she was going to the Great Western to see anyone. They would think May was a mere country bumpkin for putting up at a place that had such an old-world reputation about it, and that didn't sound up to date. Accordingly, she vaunted

May and the intimacy less than she would have done otherwise.

But when she saw Miss Meredith all minor considerations of the vain and bumptious, and even of the socially aspiring order vanished, for the Cornish girl's first words told of a distress and wrong beside which her own looked puerile.

" Ella, help me to find out the truth about Mr. Greg! I *must* find it out, now! —at once! or I shall die of shame. *Will* you help me ? "

" Yes," Ella stuttered out unsteadily. She had brought her own wrongs intending to ventilate them in the sympathetic atmosphere of a friend who had time on her hands, which she could afford to frivol away in considering them. Now, this friend had won the toss, and was already posing as the owner of a far more tragic grievance. It was hard on Ella, but as it was about Mr. Greg that the unpalatable truth had to be discovered, Ella was quite ready to aid and abet in the discovery, and resignedly let her own less definite wrongs remain in abeyance for the time.

Then May, with many diversions and interruptions from herself into paths of incident and experience that took Ella into quite a new and untried country, told her story, or rather a portion of it. She nothing extenuated as far as she was concerned, nor did she set down aught in malice to him; but she gave Ella to understand that either he was very much of a rogue, or she very much of a fool, and she meant to have a clear understanding as to which was which.

"He said he would write in a week or two, and the two weeks have passed and he hasn't written. What would you do if you were me?"

"Exactly what you'll do—*if* I were you," Ella said promptly, "but if you ask me what ¡I would do if a man served *me* so I'll tell you."

"Tell me."

"Bowl him out. He has a secret at that Norwood place, go and find it out for yourself, don't waste time in writing to his club."

"I can't think it's anything bad," May protested.

"What would you call 'bad'?" Ella asked harshly. She was in the mood to believe the worst about any man! Guy St. Austle had failed *her* (she forget that she had no claim upon him), therefore any lesser man might confidently be expected to fail any lesser woman.

" I should think it bad, very bad, if while he was pretending to me he was engaged to another girl."

" You would soon find out if that was the case if you went to the place where he doesn't want you to write to him. There must be a landlady or someone there who would be able to tell you something about him if he should happen to be out. It will be time enough after you have been to Norwood to write to his club."

" It looks dreadfully like prying into his private affairs," May said hesitatingly and despondently, but she was presently cheered and strung up by Ella remarking:

" You look upon yourself as engaged

to him, don't you? You ought to know something about his private affairs before you marry him, and as you have no father or mother to enquire into them for you you must do it for yourself."

"I don't like the idea of going alone," May admitted. For once in her life the girl was feeling shy and diffident. Or it might have been that in her prophetic soul she felt that in her pursuit of knowledge she would receive a deadly wound.

"What did you come up to town to do then?" Ella asked practically.

"I intended writing to ask him to call on me here, and then I should have had you with me, and it wouldn't have seemed such a forward and bold proceeding."

"You can have me with you at Norwood if you like. I'll go with the greatest pleasure," Ella said eagerly. It was one of her heartiest desires to find out something, especially if it were anything bad, about Mr. Greg. For she still believed that he was the man who had been the unlawful lover of her step-mother and the bane of her father's second married life.

"You *are* good to go with me. I shan't mind it half as much if I have you to back me up," May said gratefully. "You're so ready and quick, that you'll make it seem a much less out-of-the-way proceeding than I should. I should be sure to blurt out something that would be better left un-said if I had to tackle the landlady alone."

"Perhaps he may be living with his mother, or a relation. It may be his home, not lodgings only," Ella suggested.

27*

"Oh, I think if it had been his home he wouldn't have minded my writing there. But you know men are careless with their letters, and he was probably afraid of mine falling into the landlady's hands. I'm sure if it had been his home he would have spoken to me about it when we were talking about his settling down at Belhaven. You can't think how fond he is of Belhaven, Ella! It's lucky that he is, for I don't think I could have made up my mind to marry a man who didn't love Belhaven and the horses and dogs as well as I do myself. It's lucky that he does, isn't it?"

"Very lucky," Ella said laconically.

"How I long to have him back there," May resumed enthusiastically; "he enjoys the country life so thoroughly, and he'll enjoy it more than ever when he's master of everything."

" Very likely."

" There'll be no more business bothers to keep him away from me then," May resumed, pursuing her own blissful train of thought.

" What *is* Mr. Greg? What is his business?"

" I'm sure I don't know," May laughed unconcernedly; " he never talked about it to me, we had other things to think and speak about."

" It doesn't much matter what he is, as he is to be master of Belhaven. Only I wonder——" Ella paused and Miss Meredith asked quickly:

" What do you wonder at?"

" His being so reserved, with such a frank,

outspoken girl as you are, especially as he seemed so frank and outspoken himself about unimportant things."

"The truth is, I believe, we were in love with each other from the first and thought of nothing but ourselves when we were together, just ourselves and the hunting, and the horses and dogs, you know."

"I suppose that was it," Ella assented, but she did not quite mean what she said.

It was a dreary, drizzling day when they went down to Norwood, and to this circumstance they attributed a certain dejection of spirit which possessed them both when they reached their bourn in a fly. The seclusion of the lane and the smallness of the cottage made an unpleasant impression upon the mistress of Belhaven.

She did not like the idea of her hero living for ever so short a time in such a humble and out of the way place.

"I was right, he can only have lodged here," she whispered to Ella, and the next moment she had rung the bell. In a minute the door was opened by a maid-servant who stared at such unwonted visitors in undisguised astonishment.

"Is Mr. Greg staying here?" Miss Meredith asked.

"Yes, Miss, but he's not at home now."

"When is he likely to be in?" May asked less confidently.

"To dinner at seven, Miss."

"I should like to come in and write a note to him. Will you ask the land——the mistress of the house if I can do so?"

"That's Mrs. Greg, yes, Miss," the girl said

promptly ; " walk inside if you please, young ladies, and I'll call the mistress."

" It is his home, and it must be his mother," Ella murmured to May, who had grown suddenly very pale, as they were ushered into the little sitting-room which was rife with evidences of Mr. Greg's habitual occupancy. Several photographs of himself were about on the piano and mantelpiece, and a double frame held, as the pendant to the handsome Ted, one of a lady, whose melancholy beauty and glorious eyes attracted Ella's attention at once.

" This can't be his mother," May said, her lips trembling ; " it must be his sister. What a sweet face ! Why, Ella, she's like *you.*"

The door opened and the original of the sweet-faced photograph stood before the

astonished girls; but there was no sweetness in the eyes that flashed fire as they
lighted on May.

"You wish to leave a note for my—for
Mr. Greg?" she said coldly, and May
answered hurriedly:

"If you will kindly allow me. I am
Miss Meredith—May—perhaps he has
spoken of me to you."

"You are the person who wrote to him
rather more than a fortnight ago, addressing him as your 'own darling Ted,'" Mrs.
Greg said, speaking very deliberately, never
moving her eyes from the face of the now
thoroughly startled and confused girl
before her.

"I wrote to him as you say, but I am
sure he has not been base enough to show
my letter—the letter of the girl who is to be

his wife—to anyone," May began proudly, She was going on to say, "Not even to you, who may be his sister," but she was stopped by a bitter laugh and the words:

"My husband did not show me your letter, you are right there, Miss Meredith, but I found it and read it and made him reply to it with the truth that he is a married man. After that how dared you follow him here?"

She asked the question commandingly, but May was incapable of answering her. Before Mrs. Greg had uttered it the warm-hearted, proud, fearless young Cornish girl had tottered and fallen on the floor a mass of insensibility for a time.

"You are cruel, you are *brutal*," Ella flamed out fiercely; "she never knew he was married, *she* never heard it from him.

It is he who has been a blackguard, not she who is to blame."

She was down on the floor supporting her friend's head tenderly as she spoke; looking up to take a glass of water from Mrs. Greg's hand, she found that lady staring straight at her with a mixture of amazement and agony in her expression that startled the girl into exclaiming:

" Why are you looking at me so? Haven't I—yes, surely I *have*—seen you before? "

" Tell me your name? " Mrs. Greg had grown as pale as her unconscious rival, and as she spoke she staggered to a chair.

" Ella Poynter is my name," Ella said wonderingly, and then to her consternation the woman who had spoken with harshness that almost amounted to brutality to her innocent rival, broke into a storm of tears as she sprang forward, caught Ella in her arms, and showered kisses on the girl's face.

"Who are you? you frighten me," Ella stammered, and a cry of what sounded like horror broke from her when Mrs. Greg answered:

"I am your mother!"

CHAPTER VIII.

" No, no, no! don't say such a wicked thing. *My* mother died when I was quite little."

Ella poured out these words half defiantly, half appealingly ; and even as she spoke them she glanced anxiously at May Meredith, and felt thankful that the latter was still in an unconscious condition, and so unable to grasp the meaning of the awful declaration Mrs. Greg had just made.

For that it was an awful one to Ella was evident to the excited, unhappy woman who had made it. There was no attempt on Ella's part to disguise the feeling of bitter disappointment, misery, and shame which possessed her on learning that the mother whom she all her life had believed to be dead, and whose virtues and excellences she had been in the habit of vaunting to the disparagement of her step-mother, should turn out to be the erring one after all. There was neither love, sympathy, nor pity in her heart or in the expression of her face as she pushed herself away from her mother's embrace with the cruel words:

"No, no, no! don't say such a wicked thing. My mother died when I was quite little."

"I have been wrong, wrong all through, terribly wrong now to let the truth that is so terrible to you escape me," Mrs. Greg said, more to herself than to her daughter, and Ella winced at the sight of the misery

that was painted on the repulsed mother's
face, but held herself at arm's length still.

"You have been wrong to tell me such a
terrible untruth, you mean," she said with
all the severity of a young Judge; "but I
will try to forget and forgive the shock you
have given me. May, dear! you are better
now," she added gently, as Miss Meredith
raised her head and stared helplessly about
her; "try to stand up, dear, and let us get
out of this—this horrible place."

As May staggered to her feet a flood
of recollections almost overwhelmed her
again, but she struggled against it with
sufficient success to be able to say to
Mrs. Greg, who seemed to have forgotten
her existence:

"I came here under the influence of a
delusion, will you believe that? Will you

do me the justice of believing that if I had suspected he was a married man I would rather have died than have let my heart go out to him? Will you believe that I am not a bad girl, Mrs. Greg, only a mistaken one?"

"Oh, it matters very little. I have just had a worse blow than you have given me." Mrs. Greg spoke so mournfully and looked so reproachfully at Ella as she spoke that May, glancing hastily from one to the other, was struck afresh by the likeness between them and had a suspicion of the truth.

"I am sorry, very sorry that you should have more trouble than I have given you unintentionally. I wish I could do something to make you happier. Ella," she added impulsively; "trust me, tell me what this lady is to you? You are so like her, she might be your——"

"Oh! come away," Ella interrupted; "*please* come away, May; I would do anything you asked me to spare you pain and annoyance—come away."

She laid her hand on Miss Meredith's arm as she spoke, and dragged rather than led her to the door. As she passed out she cast one backward glance and shuddered as her mother opened her arms in a final, pitiful appeal for one sign of love and recognition from her child.

"I can't believe it, I *won't* believe it," she said in response; then she hurried May out, and as they got into the fly and drove off she said in an explanatory tone:

"I thought that Mrs. Greg was mad when she attacked you so shamefully; I feel sure of it now from something she said when you were fainting."

"What did she say?" May asked, and Ella, thrown off her guard by the abruptness of the question, answered:

"She pretended to be—a—a connection of mine."

"So she is, I am sure; you are so like her you might be her daughter, Ella."

"My mother died when I was quite little, so it's no use her pretending to be *that*," Ella said haughtily.

"Perhaps she didn't die," May observed musingly.

"But she did; how could Papa have married again if she didn't?" Ella said decisively. "No, the long and the short of it is that the woman is *mad*, and probably she is no more Mr. Greg's wife than she is my mother."

"Did she say she was your mother?"

"She claimed to be; if she said she was a relation of my mother's I might have looked into her claim."

Ella spoke loftily, and tried to look unconcerned. But all the time she was tingling with the deadly fear of there being truth in the mad woman's story.

"Ella, you really ought to find out the truth, whatever it may be," May said earnestly. "She is no more mad than you and I are. She is an unhappy woman, God forgive me for having added to her unhappiness, but she is not mad."

"I know if I were in your place, May, I shouldn't believe that she's Mr. Greg's wife unless I heard it from his own lips. It's only fair to him that you should hear his side of the story. She may be an intriguing woman who is trying to catch him, that

28*

I think very likely, and perhaps he may have been bothered into promising to marry her; one often hears of such things. But I don't believe she is Mrs. Greg, and I never want to hear of her again."

Unconsciously May found herself listening to these words with more consideration than she was in the habit of giving to Ella's utterances. She became thoughtful and silent, turning the possibilities which her companion had suggested over and over in her mind until they assumed the air of probabilities. After all, it was more likely that the mistress of the little Norwood cottage should be off her head sufficiently to labour under delusions concerning her relations with Ted Greg than that he should have been wicked and foolish enough to play fast and loose with

Miss Meredith, of Belhaven. Women of that time of life often were subject to delusions about men, she had heard. Very likely he had been kind and attentive to her; he had a kind, attentive manner towards most women! and she had fallen in love with him, and being a little mad had persuaded herself that she was his wife. That she should be an imbecile fool was a far more natural solution of the matter than that he should be an inveterate liar and fraud. Before she got back to the Great Western Hotel May had quite adopted Ella's view of the case, and had made up her mind to do as he had asked her, and write to him at his Club.

Ella strongly advocated this course. She longed on her own account now to see Mr. Greg, and glean from him, without committing herself, some information about the woman who had dared to claim to be her mother. Strenuously as she denied this claim even to herself, she still had a sneaking desire to have her assurance of its absolute falsity endorsed by someone who knew. If she had allowed herself to credit it, the ground on which she had stood firmly all her thinking life would have been ruthlessly cut away from under her feet. Her pride in and love for herself, her gigantic sense of the superiority of her own mother over her father's second wife, her delightful habit of insulting Mrs. Poynter by innuendo, all these would be shattered and torn away from her, if the woman calling herself Mrs. Greg were not the mad pretender Ella chose to consider her.

Once or twice May Meredith faltered in her determination to write to Ted at the Club. But when she spoke of her doubt as to the advisability of doing it to Ella, the latter laughed her scruples to scorn, and jeered at her infirmity of purpose.

"If I loved a man well enough to tumble down in a heap on the floor on merely hearing that he was married, I wouldn't give him up without letting him have a chance of clearing himself. You don't even know that he hasn't written to you? Most likely he has written, and that person has stopped his letters. She would be quite capable of doing it, as she opened and read yours to him. What do you know of her that you should take her word against his, whom you know so well?"

" Perhaps I don't know him well," May

said; "yet you're right, Ella. I have no right to think badly of him all in a moment on the mere word of a stranger!"

"Certainly not! if he is to be condemned, don't condemn him without a hearing!"

"If I write to him, and he comes, it will be dreadful to have to say to him outright, 'Ted, I have heard a horrible thing, I have been told you're a married man.'"

"Yes, I agree with you May, it would be a dreadful thing to say it out in that sledge-hammer fashion. If there's no truth in the story he would be justified in feeling enraged with you for having credited it. There are a dozen ways in which you can give him the chance of setting himself straight with you, without being brusque and abrupt."

"It's my nature to be rather brusque I'm afraid."

"You musn't be with the man you love. I'm sure Mr. Greg is a very proud man; you'll lose him if you insult him by accusing him before you give him a chance of explaining."

"I must say something about it when I see him. He will hear that I have been there and know what I have heard, and he will be justified in thinking very badly of me if I take no notice of it."

"Of course you must take notice of it—in a way. But as to his hearing that you have been there, I doubt that. She will keep him in the dark about your visit, if, as I suspect, she has deceived you. How *can* you hesitate and delay about sending

for him, May? I should be so impatient to
have it over."

"You're right, I had better know the
worst or the best as soon as possible. I
am wretched and unsettled now; after
seeing him I may be wretched still, but at
least I shall be settled."

The lines she wrote to him were brief
and non-committal. She would not
address him again as her "own darling
Ted" till she knew that he was so in very
truth, nor would she lapse into the
rigorous and severe style, and address him
as "Dear Mr. Greg," until she knew that
he deserved it. So she wrote:

"Not having heard from you as you
promised, I write to ask you to come and
see me here any time to-morrow.—Truly
yours, MAY."

He had left his Club when this letter was delivered, and gone home, where he found his wife looking very strange and unlike herself. She said nothing to him about the visitors who had called on him and found her, to their cost. Her heart was too full of bitterness and pain at having been denied and rejected by her own child for her to rouse herself to the task of telling him that she had undeceived the girl he had misled. The subject of May seemed to her to be of secondary importance now. The girl seemed a good girl, and if she was what she seemed she would never again make or accept any overtures to or from a married man, now that she knew him to be one. That episode Mrs. Greg regarded as over and done with, and she felt it would be worse

than unwise to tickle Ted's vanity, by
telling him that Miss Meredith had been
infatuated enough to follow him to town.
Moreover, she could hardly say anything
about Miss Meredith without mentioning
by whom Miss Meredith had been accompanied, and she shrank from baring
the wound her daughter had inflicted on
her before the man for whose sake she had
deserted and rendered herself unworthy of
that daughter.

It was a fact, too, though Marian Greg
hardly realised it yet, that the incident of
the morning, instead of making her turn
more clingingly and fondly to her husband, had dealt a blow to the patient,
passionate affection she had hitherto enter-
tained for him. For the first time she felt
that he had not been worth the sacrifice

she had made for him. From the beginning he had gone after strange goddesses ;
she admitted to herself now that he had
done this, and that ·she had known it and
suffered from it, even while she had still
abjectly worshipped and clung to him.
But this experience of the light in which
her own child regarded her had opened her
eyes to the magnitude of her own crime,
the fatuousness of her own folly. Now
that it was too late, she allowed her reason
to tell her the truth. He had *never* been
worth the sacrifice ! Looking at him, as
he sat opposite to her at the dinner-table,
she recognised the truth, instead of avert-
ing her mental vision and recoiling from
it. He had never been anything but
careless and selfish where she was concerned. He had taken her, and broken

her, and—tired of her! She knew it all
now, and she knew that she had deserved
it. What madness had possessed her when
she thought the world well lost for love of
such a man? He was a splendid-looking
fellow still, as "goodly to look upon" as
when she had eloped with him; but she
had never relied upon or honoured him, she
had only loved him! and all the time he
had been loving other women, and winning
their love in return. It seemed to her,
now, that it mattered very little whether
he still hankered after Miss Meredith or
not. But she would not tell him that Miss
Meredith had been to seek him out,
because that would please and make him
vainer than ever.

Her silence and abstraction annoyed him
at last, and stung him into saying :

"If you're ill I wish you'd say so, Marian, instead of sitting, looking as melancholy and resigned as a monkey at the Zoo."

"I don't feel well, and I do feel melancholy, but I can assure you I am not a bit resigned," she replied wearily. And he asked:

"What's gone wrong?—has the lodger left without paying his rent, or has the cat broken any of your best crockery? I tell you what it is, Marian, you stay in the house and mope too much. Why don't you go out and see something of your neighbours?"

"Thanks for your suggestion, but my neighbours belong to a class of which I don't want to see anything. When I go out I prefer going to see those who are poorer and more miserable than myself."

"That's your confounded pride. You might have had no end of friends by this · time if you hadn't always been so stand-off-the-grass with people."

"It never occurred to you to introduce me to any of your own friends—of the set you were in before you were married to me," she said, looking him full in the face.

"You were so sensitive at first, that if they hadn't rushed into your arms you would have thought they were slighting you. And then after a time I got out of the way of thinking about it, and now it would be devilish awkward to do it as you've kept in the background so long."

"Don't think I am blaming or reproaching you. I have felt my place to be in the background since I became the fatal means of blighting your life and my own."

" What has come over you ? " he asked, wonderingly, for this was the first time he had ever heard her speak remorsefully.

" The feeling that the beginning of the end has come," she sobbed hysterically, and he let the subject drop.

CHAPTER IX.

WITH THE STREAM.

" I will call on you at four."

This was the telegram May Meredith received from Mr. Greg in reply to her note on the following morning, and when she read it aloud to Ella, the latter said :

"It will be better for you to get it over with him alone ; however things go, it will be embarrassing for both of you to have me present, so I shall take the opportunity of going home and packing up some more of my things."

In spite of her strongly, almost fiercely, avowed disbelief in the truth of Mrs. Greg's statement that she was Ella's mother, the girl was compelled to feel that Mrs. Poynter was a less faulty woman than in her filial jealousy she (Ella) had always thought her to be. But if Mrs. Poynter were proved to be the most virtuous of her sex, if she were as absolutely above suspicion as Cæsar's wife was expected to be, Ella knew that she would never like " the woman," as she called her, one whit the better than she had done hitherto.

For "the woman" had committed the unpardonable sin of having taken unto herself the man whom the girl had idealised into the part of *the* one man in the world to be coveted. If Guy St. Austle could only be brought to see the error of his ways, if he could only be persuaded to pursue the manlier course, which Ella was quite ready to show him, of preferring herself to time-worn Mrs. Poynter, then the

29*

latter might go down to her grave un-
harassed and unhated by Ella. But!—if
" he persisted in his pernicious fidelity to
that poisonous woman," then Ella felt that
she would readily and willingly wreck them
both if possible.

Meantime she went back to her step-
mother's house armed, as she imagined, at
all points against gratifying any curiosity
Mrs. Poynter might express as to where she
(Ella) had been and whom she had seen
while she had been May Meredith's guest ;
while May remained at the hotel in a state
of alternate· longing for and dread of the
appearance of the loved but suspected one.

For in spite of the hope-against-hope
phase of feeling into which she had worked
herself up, in spite of Ella's sophistries, in
spite of the vivid recollection she had of

Ted's essentially manly and candid appearance and expression, May did suffer from the gnawing pangs of jealous suspicion. She had just made the firm resolution that as soon as she saw him she would extort the truth and the whole truth from him when he was announced ; and before she could carry her resolution into force, she found herself in his arms and felt his kisses raining down upon her face.

He was a scoundrel for acting so, and he knew himself to be one, and he was a greater scoundrel for trying to excuse himself in his own eyes by telling himself that the girl had brought this fresh unhappy complication upon herself. "If she had not followed him and sent for him and met him with a look of love that would have subjugated an anchorite he wouldn't have been blackguard enough to embrace and kiss her," he declared to himself. Even as it was he thought he was behaving rather well in releasing her quickly and saying in a cool, unembarrassed way :

"Who on earth would have thought of seeing you up here? What an erratic little woman it is to be sure!"

"It's the first time I have left Belhaven for six years. I scarcely deserve to be described as erratic."

She spoke gravely, as if she were rather hurt, which in fact she was. He felt his position was becoming uncomfortable, not to say untenable.

"Why haven't you answered my letter?" she went on, reproachfully ; "it was wrong of you, it was cruel of you, Ted, to leave such a letter unanswered."

"I did answer it; you won't understand that when a fellow is hanging between fortune and ruin he is disposed to let private matters slide, that is if he has firm reliance (as I have) on the one who shares the private matter with him."

"I wish I could *quite* believe that you were *quite* in earnest, Ted," she said uneasily; "when you left me you seemed willing to believe that I and Belhaven and all else that I have was yours as much as mine. What has changed you?—why do you speak of 'hanging between fortune and ruin,' when all that I have is yours?"

In her thorough out-and out way she had cast all thought of the "dreadful woman" who had proclaimed herself to be his wife away from her. "The idle raging of a stranger, against her knowledge of Ted!"

It could not hold out! it could not be credited for a moment longer! May began to be ashamed of herself for having listened to it at all, as she let her eyes linger lovingly on the attractive outward shell of what she believed to be a spirit that was almost bright in its brave manliness.

"I can't be mean enough to take all you have to give, without being able to offer a fair equivalent," he said with a grand, magnanimous, pride-dashed-with-humility air that was pleasing, though a trifle perplexing, to the girl, who was unprepared for this change of front.

"I don't understand," she said slowly. "I thought when you said good-bye to me at Belhaven that you understood as well as I did that there was nothing needed on your side but *you!* Now, you don't seem to understand this!—or is it that I don't understand *you?*"

He attempted to smile, but the attempt was a failure. He was beginning to realise that this unfortunate affair could not be cast into the limbo of forgotten and blotted-out bothers. He would not be permitted to tread a primrose path to freedom from May's claim upon his heart and chivalry, and no further responsibility concerning her, without proclaiming himself the rascal he was. He shrank from posing as a rascal before Miss Meredith, but if in her unsuspicious love and loyalty she drove him into a corner, there would be nothing left for him to do but to rudely rend the veil which concealed his real self from her eyes.

"Why don't you speak?" she asked

impatiently. She was in a highly strained condition, and the silence was becoming intolerable to her.

"I can't offer you a full explanation of my appearing to lag and not to fully reciprocate your sweet, womanly thoughtfulness and generosity," he said hesitatingly.

"'Thoughtfulness and generosity,' those are cold words to express what I feel for you, Ted."

She put her hand out and rested it on the back of a chair as she spoke. All the horrible misery and dread which the words of the mistress of the Norwood cottage had aroused in her mind, rushed back upon her now, causing her brain to reel and her legs to shiver. The sight of her emotion, the pain of doubting him, which was struggling with her loving trust in him, stung him to injudicious tenderness again.   Unstable as water, it was not in him to be true to either woman when out of her presence. So now, in sight of May's anguish, he cast fidelity to his wife to the winds.

"It's no use. I have tried to be prudent and keep away from you for your own sake, and now that I see you again poor Prudence hasn't a chance of being listened to. May, I wish to God I were a better fellow for your sake, but such as I am I *can't* ask you not to care for me any longer ; I can't be brave enough to ask you to forgive and forget me."

"Why should I do anything so utterly unreasonable and unpleasant?" she asked, restored to smiles and happiness at once. "If you have been unlucky or reckless about money all the more need for you to have the right to use mine as soon as possible. Ted, I believe you have been hearing tales against me? People who don't like me always say I have been my own mistress too long ever to be a good wife——"

"If the whole world spoke against you I wouldn't believe it," he interrupted eagerly.

"No! nor will I ever let myself be made miserable by a word or a hint about you. Our faith in each other is and always shall be absolute."

She glowed into beauty almost as she spoke, and he felt weaker than ever! How, after this exquisite confession of faith in him, could he ever tell her that he had a wife living who loved him and whom he professed to love?

No inspiration came to help him with an answer to this question. So he set it aside for a time and gave himself up to the present indulgence of a long happy talk with May, during which she settled their future comfortably, and he acquiesced in her arrangements.

"And now having cleared away the clouds that were between us I shall go back to Belhaven to-morrow. When will you be able to come, Ted?"

He was on the brink of taking his leave when she asked him this question, which he had been dreading the whole time.

"I may be able to run down in about a fortnight, or I may be kept three weeks."

"What keeps you, dear?" She clasped her hands over his shoulder and rested her

chin upon them, and he could not meet
her eyes—their clear, steady light seemed to
scorch him.

"What keeps me?—half a hundred
matters that you wouldn't understand."

"Shall I not understand them when we
are married?"

"It will be different then," he said
evasively, and the girl sighed and let her
hands drop from his shoulder.

"Don't send me away with a sigh, May,"
he said falteringly, catching her hand and
bending his face down towards her, but she
kept her face downcast still! He had
damped her by his evident reluctance to let
her share his confidence.

"You will come to-morrow to see me off,
won't you?"

"Of course I will! so this is not fare-

well, but only *au revoir*," he said gaily ; and
then she let him go. But though she was
to see him the next morning, and though
he had promised to follow her to Belhaven
in three weeks at the latest, she felt dreadfully depressed.

She looked round the dull private sitting-
room wistfully, unconsciously noting every
article of furniture in it. She told herself
that she was very happy in her restored
trust in her lover, and in the prospect of
so soon having him again. But at the
same time she felt that the ghosts of the
objects by which she was surrounded, and
which were being indelibly imprinted on
her memory, would start up to taunt and
haunt her at some future period of pain.

" Shall I be happy or wretched, blest or
cursed, hopeful or hopeless, when I pay my

next visit to London?" she thought, as she cast herself down on one of the saddle-back sofas, and tried to rest and stop the throbbing of her pulses before Ella came back. And when Ella came back, what, after all, had she (May) to tell beyond the bare fact that Ted had been to see her, and been affectionate and a trifle abstracted?

Now that he was out of her sight, she felt a fainter reliance on his promise to come down to Cornwall in about three weeks, and she felt an even fainter one on his making practical arrangements for their marriage when he did come. He had assented to all those propositions of hers which bore upon and forwarded the great step! But she recalled now that he had merely assented, and that she had been the only one to propose. A wave of indignation swept over her soul as she remembered this. It was not generous or thoughtful of him to leave everything to her—a girl who had neither father nor mother, brothers nor sisters, to espouse her cause and save her trouble! Perhaps it was, after all, only that he felt her to be so capable, so well able to take care of herself, that he refrained from taking the initiative. The possibility of this being the case was so soothing that she was quite able to meet Ella with a fair-weather face, and the assurance that everything " was right, quite right, between Ted and herself ! "

In spite, however, of the fair-weather face and the assurance, Ella felt pretty sure that Mr. Greg was worse than even she thought him if he ever voluntarily crossed May's path again.

For a revelation had been made to her this day, or, rather, this day she had succeeded in extracting a statement from her step-mother which at first had crushed her with shame and agony, and afterwards engendered such spite and bitterness towards most of her fellow-creatures as to be almost unnatural and altogether unscrupulous.

The girl had been primed with the intention of getting full information concerning her dead mother from Mrs. Poynter, without betraying to the latter that she (Ella) had the faintest suspicion of her mother's fate being other than it had always been represented to be to her, namely, a brief life of married happiness and an early death. But in her eagerness and excitement she tripped in her carefully pre-arranged speech, and instead of saying:

"Did you know anything of Mrs. Greg when you married my father?" she asked:

"Do you think my mother ever knew that Mr. Greg we met at Trelyn Towers?"

She could not keep a tremor of anxiety and pain out of her voice as she asked this, and in a moment all the womanly tenderness that was rarely dormant in Mrs. Poynter's nature woke up.

"My dear child, who has been cruel enough to prompt you to ask such a question? Let Mr. Greg and everything connected with him be blotted out from your memory. He is not a good friend for either woman or girl. Forget that you ever knew him."

"I'm not likely to be able to forget that, for he is going to be married to my friend, May Meredith; but a terrible woman, who

30*

must be mad, told May and me yesterday,
when we went to look him up at his lodgings, that she was his wife and my mother.
Preposterous, wasn't it?"

Ella spoke the last sentence with jaunty
uneasiness, for Mrs. Poynter had covered
her face with her hands. It must all come
out now, she knew. The sad secret which
had only been made known to her after
her own marriage, the story of the discovery, and divorce, and disgrace, must all
be made known, not only to the innocent
child, but to Guy St. Austle. And he, with
his high code of morality, with his preju-
dice against marrying a woman who had
been another man's wife, what would he
think of her now? He would regard her
union with the husband of the divorced
woman as illegal, as unsanctioned either by

God or the Law. Still, she would not secure her own happiness at the cost of any further lying or deception.

"Your mother was unhappy enough to meet Mr. Greg after she married your father. She was very young. Think *very* gently of her, Ella! She has been very heavily punished. You, her only child, were taken from her, and now it seems that the man for whom she sacrificed herself is false to her."

Ella held her white face up as proudly as ever, but her eyes flashed like angry stars, and her lips trembled.

"She is my mother, then?"

"She is your mother. I vowed that I would keep all knowledge of her from you; your father made me do it, but I was wrong. She *is* your mother, and all these years she has been deprived of her daughter's love. You must make up to her for these lost years now, Ella; you must give her all the love that has been withheld from her all this time."

" Does Mr. St. Austle know anything about this?" Ella asked coldly.

"He knows nothing—yet."

" I know what his views are," Ella cried triumphantly; " he will think worse of you than he will of me——"

" Ella, he will never think badly of you, or hardly of your poor mother. Don't be so bitter, my poor child!"

" But he holds that those whom God has joined together man may not put asunder, I know he does. He will look on my mother as my father's wife still; so what will he think of you? You had better let things go on as they are, and keep the secret still."

" May all the misery that may come for having kept it so long fall on me. I only ask one thing of you, Ella, be kind to your mother now you have found her."

" I will never see her again if I can help it," the girl said vindictively. "I have loved her dead, and *better* than *you*, too long for me to humble myself by standing by her side now that I know she's alive and worse than you. I've always hated and despised you, I've always put my mother high above you! I hate you more than ever now that I can't despise you any longer."

Her voice had risen higher and higher during the delivery of this vicious tirade. The last words were rather shrieked than spoken, for the poor wilful girl had to struggle with the sobs that were almost choking her. As she paused, panting with rage and shame, Guy St. Austle came forward, asking in an angry and astonished tone:

"What is the meaning of this? Are you mad to speak to Mrs. Poynter, who has been like a mother to you, in this insulting and cruel way, Ella?"

"Like a mother to me!" the girl repeated scornfully; "how I wish I had never had a mother!" Then the pent-up floods of tears burst out, and she cried till her passion was over.

CHAPTER X.

IT was within ten minutes of the time for the departure of the train by which May Meredith and Ella Poynter were to travel down into Cornwall, and still Mr. Greg had not put in his promised appearance. May's spirits had been declining gradually as time slipped by, and there was no sign of her lover, and Ella's had been as gradually rising. She felt prophetically sure that if he allowed May to start without seeing her that outraged love and pride would induce May to break with him definitely, and so spare Ella the necessity of exposing his perfidy and her mother's dishonour. She shrank from the thought of doing this with a feeling of smarting shame that was cruelly hard to bear. But sharp and severe as the strain was, the girl bore up under it with outward composure that would have been heroic had the feeling that prompted it been more filial. Her one desire now was to get away to a place where no one knew or even suspected her secret. In London she would always be liable to meet either Mrs. Poynter or Guy St. Austle, however sedulously she avoided their home and their haunts. But down at Belhaven no one knew anything about her that would justify them in either looking down upon or pitying her. Pity was as obnoxious to her as contempt in her young, arrogant, hard frame of mind. So she panted to be off to a place where nothing was known that could cause either feeling, and prayed that the time would fly faster as earnestly as May did that it would stand still till *he* came.

The inevitable moment for starting arrived, and there was no Ted to speed her on her way with words and looks of love. They had a carriage to themselves fortunately, for when the train had fairly started May could not any longer bear her pain and mortification in silence. The tears came up and dimmed her last view of the platform, and as they steamed out of the station she bared her wound.

"How can he have been so cruel as to let me go without seeing me again?" she asked mournfully, and Ella, whose most earnest current aspiration was that neither she nor May might ever cast eyes on or hear of the man who had ruined her mother's life again, said decisively :

" He is cruel as you say, cruel and heart-lessly insulting. I hope you will never give another thought to him, May. I hope he will die before he ever tries to come near you again."

" You took a very different view of his conduct yesterday," May said wonderingly. " You begged me then to trust him, and be deaf to everything that I might hear against him. You're not consistent."

" Yesterday he hadn't treated you with indifference and contempt to my know-ledge. To-day he has done so ; he couldn't show you more plainly that he doesn't love you, and doesn't want you, than he has done this morning."

" I feel that."

"Then throw all thought of and kind feeling for him away. Don't be such a *soft* as to go on caring for a man who seems to take delight in showing that he doesn't care for you."

"Don't, don't," poor May cried, putting up her hands as if to avert a blow. "You don't know what this is to me—you don't know how he has seemed to love me—you don't know how he has *said* he loves me. I can't think that it's all over—that he has gone out of my life, that he's not *my* Ted any longer—yet."

"He's done his best to make you feel it," Ella said, with the philosophical fortitude one girl is apt to display about the love troubles of another.

"He must be ill, or some accident must have happened to him," May said

piteously, then instantly she added remorsefully :

"There's no comfort in that thought
though. I'd rather bear anything than
that he should be ill or suffering."

"If a man served me such a shabby
trick I should wish him every evil under
the sun," Ella said, thinking spitefully of
Guy St. Austle as she spoke. "I should
wish him to marry a wife who would bore
him to death in a week, and make his
home unhappy; I should wish everything
he undertook to fail——"

"Not if you loved him," May interrupted, "you'd wish him, as I do Ted,
every blessing under the sun. It would
hurt me more than I am hurt already if I
thought he wasn't happy."

"If I were like you, going to a beautiful

home and beautiful horses and dogs, all of
my very own, with no one to interfere with
me in any way, I'd never give a thought to
a man even if he worshipped me, and as for
wasting a bit of feeling on one who didn't,
I should as soon think of cutting my throat.
Do be happy, you lucky girl, you have
everything to make you so. No relations
to worry you——"

"No, I am terribly alone in the world,
and yesterday I seemed to have everything," May said sadly, but Ella's words
bore a certain sort of fruit. For the
remainder of the journey May did try to
think and speak about Belhaven, and to
Ella's intense relief did refrain from further
mention of her fickle and forgetful lover.

The following day's post did not bring
her what she had ardently hoped for, if not

confidently expected—a letter, namely, from
Mr. Greg, explaining his conduct. What
misery the non-fulfilment of her hope
caused the girl, no one but herself knew.
She spent the evening alone, locked in her
bed-room, and when she met Ella at
breakfast the next morning, there were
signs of such suffering on her face as are
caused sometimes by witnessing the death-
throes of someone most dearly loved, and
Ella understood that the subject of May's
false love was not to be mentioned between
them.

For a week May busied herself within
he limits of her own house and grounds.
At the end of that time she proposed
driving over to Trelyn Towers, and after
that she resumed all her former occupations
and habits, and life flowed on at Belhaven

as if Ted Greg had never been there to disturb its current.

There was a little uneasiness mixed with the pleasure with which the St. Austles welcomed back their formerly buoyant-natured young neighbour. They were too well-bred, as well as too kind-hearted, to express curiosity as to what had taken her up to town so suddenly, and what had sent her home in so subdued a mood. But in their own minds they both felt that Ted Greg had more to do with the suddenness of the movement and the sadness of the mood than met the eye. She never mentioned their late guest herself, and intuition taught them he was a topic better avoided. So his name remained unspoken in her hearing for so long a time, that at last she hungered for the sound of it in order to test by her sensations whether she had reached that stage of almost stony endurance which she had set herself to attain.

That he was rarely absent from her thoughts during her waking hours was painfully true. She could not control herself to cease from conjecturing what it was that had made him play her false. That he was, if not married to, at the least very seriously entangled with the woman who had proclaimed herself his wife on the occasion of May's visit to the Norwood cottage, the latter could no longer doubt. But why had he been brutal enough to win her heart, pose as a free man, and bring this awful disgrace upon her of having loved a married man? Why had he been deceitful in his desperate wickedness up to the very last, the last fatally, frantically, degradingly happy day when he had come to the hotel and embraced her in a way that made her shudder now as she thought of it.

She could not help conjecturing continually why he had done these things, any more than she could be blind to the phantasmagorial semblance of his face and form which would unceasingly rise up and blot out everything else from her sight. When she had been perfectly happy in her belief in being honourably engaged to him, it had annoyed her sometimes that she could not at her heart's will conjure up a vision of him as he had looked under certain conditions that had been peculiarly becoming to him in her eyes. But now that she had lost him for ever, he was constantly recurring vividly in his habit as he

31*

lived, and with all that had most attracted her in his expression strongly depicted. A thousand times when she was striving to absorb herself in the excitements of a hunting day she would see him going with dashing steadiness at the stiffest bit in the fence in front of her, and sailing over it with exquisite skill. If she could only have seen him at home for a few days perhaps he would not have been so glorified in her after - thoughts and visions of him! But this was a spectacle she had been spared hitherto, and so she could neither forget, despise, nor become indifferent to the vivid presentment which her memory gave of him.

The prospect of lapsing into a state of lonely old-maidenhood had no terrors for May Meredith. It rarely has for girls who are well endowed with this world's goods.

But the idea of never seeing Ted Greg again, save in some casual, cool, and constrained way, made her sick. She knew that seeing him would only set bleeding afresh those wounds of disappointment, mortification, and love that was still dear. She knew that if she experienced one throb of pleasure at the sight of him, she would be as weak as she was wicked. And yet, oh! how desperately she did long to see Ted again, against all the dictates of prudence, reason, and propriety—against even the certain knowledge she had that a meeting with him would only intensify the misery she was already enduring.

She had one solitary little bit of comfort, she knew that if there were gossippings and speculations about her none of them would reach her ears. She had been a Bird of

Freedom so long that now, when she had been winged, there was no one sufficiently audacious in the circle of her acquaintances and friends to tell her that her wound had been observed. But one day, when she dropped in to afternoon tea with Lady St. Austle, an unconscious hand probed the wound deeply.

She found quite a little family party assembled in Laura's drawing-room; Mrs. Robert Davis and her children in an effervescent and jubilant state, for which she was at a loss to account until Lady St. Aubyn explained the situation to her.

"We are having a gala day amongst ourselves. My brother, Mr. Davis, perhaps you may have heard how terribly he was treated and how *fearfully* he has suffered through unscrupulous speculators—has had his affairs righted."

"You should say that he has righted them himself, Laura," Mrs. Robert Davis interposed with fussy loyalty. "No one can tell how he has struggled and sacrificed himself, Miss Meredith, living away from all his home comforts in nasty common lodgings, separated from his wife and children, and with such an *undeserved* stigma on his name. I consider he has been heroic, and now Laura speaks of his affairs 'having been righted,' as if someone else had done it for him."

"Well, they are righted," Laura said with patient sweetness, though she had been considerably curtailed in many of her justifiable expenditures lately in order that, at her entreaties, her husband should advance "just one more thou' to poor Robert"; "and he's coming down to stay with us for a few days, and when he goes away I'm thinking half my occupation will be gone, for Anna and the children will want to go with him, and I shall have no more pleasant looking-after-them duty to do."

"My dear Laura, you could not expect, you could not even hope, that you would always have us at your gates to fall back upon during your hours of idleness."

"I'm certain if I had been Lady St. Austle I should never have hoped it, whatever I might have expected," May put in sharply, but Mrs. Davis's mental hide was unpenetrated by the sting.

"Naturally you wouldn't," she said with complacent graciousness. "My husband has the first claim on me, and Laura must, in parting with us, make a sacrifice to her brother in return for all he has sacrificed for her. *Such* a wedding as he gave her, Miss Meredith! *You*, living down here in your pretty, retired little place, can have no conception of the scale on which it was done. I don't think we shall return to Norwood," she added loftily to Laura, and Laura, with a conscience void of all inten tention of giving offence, replied hastily :

" Oh, no, I hope not, Anna ; it would be too horrid for you to go back and live in a humble way in a neighbourhood where you had such a jolly house and establishment, and—and I don't think Walter would help you any longer if you did it," she added timidly.

" Walter help us !" Mrs. Robert Davis

repeated with fine scorn. "You will
find when your brother comes that he will
not rely much on Sir Walter St. Austle's
help. Oh, he's been very kind, and so have
you, Laura, to me and the children; glad
you must be to feel that you've been able
to make any return at all for all the years
you lived with us, but when Robert comes
you'll find——"

"Mr. Davis," the butler announced, and
May Meredith saw a furtive-eyed, fugitive-
mannered, self-conscious man come in with
a hurried, deprecatory air that repelled her
at once.

But sweet Lady St. Austle gave him a
warm, welcoming, sisterly kiss, and his wife
hailed him as if he had been the lost tribe
of Israel, and she were the explorer who
would receive the blue ribbon of the

Exploration Society for having found him. So May did not escape at once, as instinct warned her to do.

"Surely I have seen this young lady before!" he said presently, when the family embracings and gratulations had ceased for a time. He stared hard at Miss Meredith, and a vague sensation of uneasiness beset her at once.

"I can't recall having had the pleasure of meeting you," she said, giving a little gulp over the polite part of her speech.

"It wasn't exactly a 'meeting'; fact is, I saw you from the parlour window of my lodgings in Norwood; you came with Miss Poynter one day to call on Mrs. Greg, or rather I should say on Mr. Greg, for the servant told me you asked for him. By the way, Laura, Walter knows Greg I understand, he's been staying here he tells me. An uncommonly fine-looking, nice fellow he is too."

"But our Mr. Greg isn't a married man," Lady St. Austle was beginning uneasily, when her brother interrupted her with a coarse laugh.

"He's a very much married man, my dear Laura, only the lady always keeps very much in the background, though why she should do so I'm sure I can't conceive, for she's a perfect lady and a very handsome woman into the bargain. Miss Meredith will bear me up in saying this I'm sure."

"And I'm sure we don't want to hear anything about Mrs. Grey or Mrs. Anybody, else, and you only just come back to us, Robert," his wife interposed with a mixture of jealousy and affection for which May was inclined to hurl blessings at her head, as it diverted attention from the place in Mr. Davis's narrative which he had forced her (May) to occupy. Under cover of the fatuous denials which he poured forth as to his ever having "looked at any other woman since parting with his Anna," May made her escape without being called in a friendly way to account for her suppressed knowledge of and visit to Mrs. Greg.

CHAPTER XI.

WHEN Ella had stormily departed from Mrs. Poynter's borders that day there was a very full explanation between that lady and her lover. As compassionately as she could, Mabel told the story of her predecessor's decline and fall, and as patiently as he could Guy St. Austle listened to it.

"This was the reason of my holding aloof from you all those years, Guy. I knew it went sorely against the grain with you that you should be in love with a widow. That I should be the widow of a man whose first wife was still alive would shock you too much I feared."

" I would rather it hadn't been the case," he admitted, and the admission stung her.

" As it is the case, perhaps you would like to be released," she said quietly, but the tears that had been in her eyes a moment before were dried by the heat of the blood that rushed up to her face in a wave of hurt feeling.

He took her hand and lifted it to his lips.

"We belong to each other now, Mabel, we must accept and endure each other's errors of judgment and of action."

" I felt that you would regard my having been the wife of a man whose divorced wife was still alive as an unpardonable sin. I regarded it as one myself when first I knew it."

" You didn't know it until it was too late to draw back——"

"Too late to draw back? Why, Guy, I didn't know it till I had been married more than a year."

"Then it's a mere shadow which has stood between us," he cried heartily; "what you did in ignorance was neither sin, fault, nor folly. My own darling Mabel, how could I have been such a fool as to suppose anything else for a moment? But what a lot of time we have wasted, because you hadn't the courage to tell me all this five years ago."

"And I've kept the secret to no effect after all, for Ella has been cruelly en-, lightened by the very one who ought to have spared the poor child. And yet, Guy, I can't help feeling so bitterly sorry for poor Mrs. Greg. To have her own child shrink from her, and disown her. It's too hideously unnatural. I would give a great deal to be able to do something to comfort her, poor woman!"

"It's a case that doesn't admit of much comfort, I'm afraid. Greg is hardly the fellow for whom the world is well lost by a woman. The very fact of his swaggering about at such houses as Trelyn while she's left out in the cold in a cottage at Norwood shows that he has no consideration for her. His passion has spent its novel force, and the poor victim of it is left half her time in solitude to reflect on her own imbecility. I tell you what we must do though, Mabel, we must put Walter and Laura on their guard against Greg. He mustn't be let go on making love to May Meredith."

"Don't interfere, Ella will put May Meredith on her guard; don't make it more public than is needful," Mrs. Poynter pleaded. "I am sure we may rely on Mr. Greg's aversion to trouble and annoyance for keeping him away from Trelyn. His wife will have told him that she has recognised her daughter, and he will put two and two together, and find it pleasanter to keep out of your way and mine. Walter and Laura needn't know anything of the story in which I am mixed up, to my sorrow and regret."

"I don't like concealments," Guy said, shaking his head dubiously; but as he even more disliked the idea of Mabel's share in the drama becoming known to his own family, he consented to become accessory to one for once.

"Besides," he said in reply to his own conscience, which pricked him a bit in the matter, " it would be ghastly humiliating for poor May to have it known in her own neighbourhood that she has been made such a fool of. And Walter can never hold his tongue. Mabel is distinctly right. We owe it to May to give as little publicity to the unfortunate affair as possible."

Having arrived at this convenient conclusion and abided by it, he was rather annoyed and surprised some time after at getting a letter from his brother, in which the latter said :

" Robert Davis has turned up here fat and well-looking, and rather disposed to think that we ought all to do our level best daily and hourly to indemnify him for some trifling disagreeables he experienced while he was playing hide-and-seek, after having

32*

defrauded everyone. He has made a pile again, and, thank God, he and his tribe are going to America, to wallow in splendour under a new name I presume. He gives us the intelligence that Ted Greg has a wife; I suppose poor Ted married beneath him in his salad days, as the lady is kept completely in the background. Love to your wife; I am sorry to say Laura is not very well, and as there is scarlet fever about I'm a bit uneasy.

"Your affectionate brother,

"WALTER."

This letter was received by the happy pair, while they were spending their honeymoon soberly in the Ardennes, where Guy was laying the scene of a romantic drama of modern French country life, and Mabel was realising the truth that there is very little romance in real life after the early glow of youth is past.

*   *   *   *   *

"I could be *almost* happy again if that dreadful Mr. Davis would go away for ever," May Meredith would constantly say to herself, after having been brought into forced contact with the gentleman in question. With what seemed to her like brutal maliciousness, he would refer to "that occasion when he had caught a glimpse of her through the parlour window," or dwell with bated breath for fear his wife should hear him on Mrs. Greg's fine figure and good looks. In reality there was neither brutality nor malice in these reminiscences. Only Mr. Davis loved to talk of himself in these days, to make up for the long

spell of verbal discretion he had been
obliged to observe while at the Norwood
cottage. It did not occur to him that
anyone could be uninterested in anything
that interested him, and Mrs. Greg, with
her saddened beauty and singularly dull
and unsocial life, had interested him
greatly.

"Have you any idea who she was?" he
asked May one Sunday, when the whole
party, St. Austles, Davises, Ella, and herself,
were walking back from church to lunch at
Trelyn Towers.

"I have never speculated about her; I
never heard of her before that day, and I've
never heard of her since. And now, Mr.
Davis, as you have forced the subject on me
again, I will tell you plainly I would rather
not discuss it."

"Painful is it? I'm sorry to have offended you, but——"

"Not painful, only tedious," May interrupted. "Can't you understand that one of one's most unimportant little actions becomes a scourge if it's perpetually being picked up and hurled at one?"

"You needn't be afraid, I won't say anything before them," he said, lowering his voice mysteriously, and jerking his thumb backwards over his shoulder to indicate the ones he referred to. "Greg isn't the only man who knows a pretty girl when he sees one. I don't blame him! I've an eye for beauty myself, but mum's the word about that before Anna, and mum shall be the word about the Gregs before the others now that I know."

He only meant to be jocular after the

fashion of an underbred man, but the
assumption of being in her confidence, and
the leering look of odious familiarity
punished poor May for the unintentional
sin she had committed in loving her neighbour's husband before she knew him to be
such sufficiently. Angry, defiant, disdain-
ful words rose to her lips, but she dared
not let them be spoken, she dared not defy
this man whom she despised to insinuate
his worst and lower her in the eyes of her
old friends. She was being made to come
off her pedestal for Ted Greg's unworthy
sake, and no mistake.

After this, being idle to a certain extent
now, and being egotistical always, he fell
into the habit of calling frequently on Miss
Meredith, assuming that he and she had
sympathies and sufferings in common. He

did not exactly say so, but he implied that
he had been extremely efficacious in con-
soling Mrs. Greg during her husband's
frequent absences. He would dwell at
length on the fastidious care Mrs. Greg had
always bestowed upon the preparation of
his food, and would then sigh in a way that
May felt was intended to show her how
deeply he deplored that his Anna should
look like a cook and still be unable to rise
to those scientific heights of cookery which
Mrs. Greg had scaled so easily. He would
sink his voice to a whisper if Ella came
into the room when he was blunderingly
torturing Miss Meredith, and change the
subject with a palpable and elaborate effort
that naturally made Ella think they had
been discussing her unfavourably.

"How can you endure that talkative,

gossiping, podgy man?" Ella said one day when the palpable and elaborate effort had been more than usually pronounced.

"I want to keep him in a good temper while he's here—the beast!" May said, begining her sentence abjectly, and finishing it furiously.

"But why should you want to keep him in a good temper wherever he is?" Ella said, with the injudicious curiosity that generally reaps a slap in the face for the one who has betrayed it.

"Why? because if you will know, he saw me that unlucky day I called at the cottage in Norwood, where my happiness and pride were battered down and trampled in the dust!" May answered, with unusual vehemence. Whereupon Ella shrugged her shoulders after the manner of one who desires to dismiss a subject, and said carelessly :

" Those Gregs are a couple of im-postors. I never told you before, but I find from my step-mother, Mrs. St. Austle, that handsome Ted Greg, as he is called, really is the husband of the woman we saw there."

" The lady who said she was your mother ? " May enquired.

Ella's mobile face grew fiery and fierce in a moment.

" We mean the same person," she said drily. " Why should you hurt my feelings by reminding me of her false pretences ? "

" I didn't intend doing anything so meanly vindictive ! " May retorted warmly. " Only, Ella ! *if* you knew what it was to smart under such a cruel insult as Mr. Greg has put upon me you would understand at my marvelling at your rejection of a mother's claims before you had enquired into them. If I had a mother to turn to and love now, I shouldn't ask what place she had come from, or why she had neglected me so long. I should pray for her love and sympathy, and give her mine *so* fully."

"So would I if I didn't happen to have known all my life that my real mother died when I was a baby," Ella said obstinately.

"Did she die—are you sure of that?" May persisted. "Ella, I have heard things about Mrs. Greg from this obnoxious man, Mr. Davis, that convince me she is no common-place woman neglected by her husband because he is repenting himself of having married beneath him. She is *a lady* with a sad story, I'm sure. Do enquire into that story, Ella, and relieve her sadness if you can!"

"I have no vocation for playing the part of comforter to women who have made fools of themselves for the sake of a handsome face and a selfishly debonair manner," Ella said defiantly, and May felt that she was being included in the class whom Ella declared she had no intention of befriending. A less generous nature than May's would have resented this, but when Ella was most unbearable in her arrogance and heartlessness, Miss Meredith never forgot that the motherless girl had claims upon her which only another motherless girl could fully understand and respond to. So the subject being a sore one between them, May suffered it to drop again till the smart of it should cease.

Very shortly a fresh impetus was given to interests that centred nearer home. The fever which had been virulent for some time in the lowest and least sanitary localities in the neighbourhood, had crept upwards and stricken Lady St. Austle, and in a moment of thoughtlessness her distressed husband came down to speak of his sorrows and anxieties to his two girl-friends at Belhaven. When he had been there once there could be no danger to them in his coming again, they both argued. Accordingly, against his better judgment and sense of what was right and prudent, he would carry the latest bulletins of poor Laura's state to them in person, always providing that they should meet him in the open air, and pathetically refusing to shake hands with them at meeting or parting.

After a time Lady St. Austle's state became critical, and then Walter glued himself to the house in which she was lying in a state of delirium, or to the terraces immediately around it. No more personally conveyed bulletins to Belhaven now; only a few words, four or five times a day, scratched on a scrap of paper, and read by Ella before it had been fumigated according to scientific principles. At first there was merely a feeling of true womanly anxiety to hear how the suffering woman was bubbling up in Ella's heart, and making her regardless of precautions and careless of consequences. But after a brief while Ella became conscious that there was the exaltation of a sensation of heroism in her action. To know that she was the chosen repository daily of this man's desperately loving fears and anxious dreads regarding his beautiful wife, made the girl who had been slighted by the man's less important brother feel of more consequence in her own eyes than she had felt since Guy St. Austle had rebuffed her.   This knowledge intensified and deepened her satisfaction in being near to " poor Sir Walter," when he gave her to understand that unless she gave him the one gleam of light which a note of sympathy from her would send through the dark clouds of misery, uncertainty and anxiety which encompassed him, those clouds would envelop and destroy him utterly.   How after this could she refuse to receive and respond to those poisonous little scraps of paper which carried the germs of the disease to hitherto undefiled and unaffected Belhaven ?

Perhaps she never asked the question, How could she refrain from doing this? from anyone. Perhaps had she done so and had the reply been antagonistic to her desires, she would have disregarded the advice. Perhaps she never gave a thought to anyone or anything saving the man who was turning to her for solace in the midst of his great distress. At any rate her whole nature softened, and grew more tender and more true in these days, and the thought that she was being of use and comfort to him in his grave trouble made her braver, better and more buoyant than she had ever been before. For the first time she was of *use* to someone. Her step-mother had tried always to have been of use to her (Ella) and had failed in being so through the girl's own perversity. May

Meredith had been more than a sister in kindness and consideration, but Ella had failed to discern that she could give anything in return to this friend who seemed to want nothing of her, and who was so well endowed with worldly goods. While, as for the throng of acquaintances and so-called friends by whom she had been surrounded in " society," there had never been time for her to give a thought to their needs, and even had she done so she would in her artificial selfishness have questioned why she should be called upon or expected to supply them.

Therefore it was like water in a dry land when her arid little heart discovered that it could pour balm into the strained, hot, anxious one of Sir Walter St. Austle. She had literally no ulterior views. She scarcely looked beyond the hour at which her sympathetic letters or presence solaced him. She would have recoiled in horror from herself if the idea of Lady St. Austle's death and any possible benefits accruing to herself from it had occurred to her. And yet! and yet whenever she looked beyond the time in which he could be with her constantly it was all black darkness and utter desolation.

END OF VOL. II.